KNITTED AND KNIFED

A KNITTY KITTIES MYSTERY

TRACEY DREW

Copyright © 2020 by Tracey Drew

All rights reserved.

No part of this book may be reproduced in any form or by any electronic or mechanical means, including information storage and retrieval systems, without written permission from the author, except for the use of brief quotations in a book review.

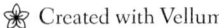 Created with Vellum

Wanted: Cat mum to manage a yarn store, corral two curious cats, all the while being tangled up in murderous mayhem and mystery.

A smart woman would dump her cheating ex, move from the city, and give herself a chance for a well-deserved do-over. A smarter woman—smarter than me, anyway—wouldn't jump out of that same frying pan and return to Cape Discovery, a seaside village where her family is the nuttiest of all the nut-ball residents.

I'm a former high school counsellor, middle-child peace-maker, and current curator of lots of squishy/fuzzy goodness at my granddad's little yarn store. *Temporary* assistant. Until I decide what to do with the rest my life. There's only one knotty problem to untangle first. The knife sticking out of the most unpopular man in town, and the police detective trying to *pin the murder on the donkey*—otherwise known as my younger brother. With a pair mischievous cats determined to be underfoot and a craft group of Serial Knitters and Happy Hookers wanting the inside scoop, a girl could lose her mind. And if the killer has their way, maybe even my life...

Tessa Wakefield has her hands full juggling a cozy craft store, her crazy family, and two men who'd rather poke out their eyes than describe themselves as cute. Which they totally are. Cute, charismatic, and occasionally on her mind when she's not stumbling over dead bodies and using her newfound sleuthing skills to track down murderers. Lucky she's an excellent multi-tasker because digging beneath Cape Discovery's surface can unearth secrets that kill.

ALSO BY TRACEY DREW

Knitty Kitties Mysteries

Knitted and Knifed
Purled and Poisoned
Hanks and a Hitman

FREE BOOK!

Want to read the prequel of Kit and Pearl's first crime-solving adventure? Click here to sign up to my newsletter and I'll send you a FREE e-copy of Balls & Bones!

ONE

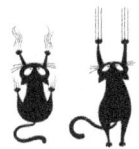

HAVE you ever reached a milestone in your life where you've thought: *This is it; I've gone from being a successful thirty-five-year-old school counselor to a woman sans home and a man, surrounded by yarn and two spoiled, high-maintenance cats.*

Well I have, and it wasn't when I caught Jared, my boyfriend of ten years, with his personal trainer after my beloved nana's funeral. Nope. My current sad existence became apparent when I entered the kitchen of my new home and spied on the counter, a chubby feline wedged inside a pastry box.

Loud munching noises filled the room.

Perhaps I should hit pause to explain who I am and how I came to catch a gluttonous cat scoffing expensive baked goods.

Hi, I'm Tessa Wakefield. A woman scorned, who fled the big city lights of Auckland to return her small New Zealand hometown. And the bosom of her family. Her slightly nutball family, but a loving family, nonetheless.

While my two older sisters and their families lived elsewhere in the country, my parents, younger brother, and paternal grandparents remained long-term Cape Discovery residents.

Except now, I have only one grandparent left. We lost Nana Dee-Dee to a massive stroke two months ago, and Granddad Harry needed us all, nutty or not, to help him adjust to the gaping hole created by her absence. As the youngest sister and the only female Wakefield sibling without a brood of kids—and with a significant other who preferred the company of his personal trainer—moving into my grandparents' spare room seemed the obvious, most helpful choice.

As a temporary measure, of course.

Just until Harry figured out what he wanted to do with the yarn store that he and Nana Dee-Dee had owned for nearly forty years.

Over those years, Nana Dee-Dee had turned Unraveled into a craft addict's paradise. Breezy and light-filled during the summer, and a cozy, welcoming haven in winter. And it would break the last fragment of Harry's shattered heart to sell the store and the two-bedroom apartment they'd lived in above it. To honor my nana, the least I could do over the busy summer season was keep Harry and Unraveled functioning. Not in the charming old-school style that made Nana Dee-Dee a much-loved local icon, but in more of a *don't worry; I've got this* trial-and-error kind of way.

So far, I'd coped with the day-to-day running of the store. While Harry managed the admin side of things, all I had to do was point yarn-o-holics to the shelf of alpaca fiber blends or ring up a purchase of rainbow-colored merino. Luckily, most customers knew what they wanted, and I spoke enough craft-ish to sound like a professional. I'd even convinced Harry to restart the Thursday night Crafting for Calmness classes, with me taking the lead.

Don't laugh—my nana taught me to knit the moment my chubby little hands could grasp a pair of knitting needles.

While there'd been plenty of crafting when Nana Dee-Dee was alive, calmness tended to be waylaid by a free-for-all of gossip, friendly rivalry between the group's knitters and crocheters, and snacks. Lots of yummy snacks. Such as the much-coveted, delicious pastries from Disco's Bakery.

Yes, the very same pastries one of Nana Dee-Dee's jet-black cats was now scoffing. And I didn't need to see the culprit's face; I recognized his chubby hindquarters.

"Kit!"

The hindquarters wriggled, and his tail flicked in agitation...but the munching sounds from inside the box only increased in speed.

"You little mother...I mean...mohair-flecking glutton!"

Even mid-rant, I was mindful of Harry next door in the living room. My granddad insisted his adult grandkids called him 'Harry,' and having been a cop for his entire working life, he claimed he'd heard enough cursing on the job so didn't want to hear it from his family. We were strongly encouraged to rise above gutter-talk. But one thing we Wakefields were good at was appearing to abide by rules while actually finding creative ways to get around, under, or through them.

I raced across the kitchen and whipped open the box lid.

Two jungle-green eyes blinked up at me. A pink tongue flicked out to swipe a clot of cream off a furry lip. Kit, the boy half of Nana Dee-Dee's devilish duo, kept his stocky paws right where he'd planted them—one in the center of an apricot Danish, the other on a custard-scrolled delight I'd personally had my eye on. He gave me a querying, "*purrrrt?*"

A *hello, human, can I help you?* response.

To add insult to injury, he slowly rose from his hunkered-down-to-feast position, displayed four licorice jellybean toes, and proceeded to lick custard from between them.

"Kit. You know those weren't for you," I wailed.

Because I was that kind of *inherited by default* cat-staff. The kind convinced that cats understand everything we say but choose to react only to the things that interest them.

Or benefit them.

Or entertain them.

Call me insane, but I shot devil eyes at Kit for a moment, waiting for an apology.

I got a bored yawn instead.

Then he jumped off the kitchen counter—he was surprisingly agile for such a furry fatty—and sashayed into the living room. No doubt to join Harry on his La-Z-Boy so they could watch *The Bachelorette* and criticize the contestants.

Sure enough, Harry soon piped up with, "Can I steal you for a moment?" then laughed. His big belly laugh that, even though I was as mad as an alpaca with an unexpected military buzz cut, still gave me the warm fuzzies.

Of course, warm fuzzies wouldn't replace the cat-chewed pastries meant for this evening's Crafting for Calmness.

I'd only left the store unattended for a minute while I

snuck upstairs for my own boredom snack. However, the salted pretzels would have to wait until after an emergency run back to Disco's.

"Harry"—had to raise my voice over the excitable females OMG'ing on the TV—"I'm going into town to pick up some more snacks."

"What happened to the ones I bought earlier?" he hollered back.

With a sigh, I dumped the whole box into the trash. I poked my head around the curved archway that divided kitchen and living room. "Kit happened. You left them on the counter instead of hiding them in the pantry."

"I did? Don't remember doing that." Harry scratched a finger under today's choice of a purple-and-orange striped knitted beanie, releasing a flyaway tuft of snowy hair. My granddad needed a haircut and a better excuse than 'I forgot.' Because, although in his early eighties, the man was whip-smart and only pretended to forget things to tease his wife.

Who would've had conniptions at me serving a store-bought packet of chocolate chip cookies. The idea had crossed my mind as an easy solution.

"Say hello to Jules from me while you're there." Harry shot me an *innocent until proven guilty* grin then toggled up the TV volume to drown out any snarky response to his blatant attempt at matchmaking.

Gah!

Mentally throwing up my hands, I left him and the smirking black menace curled up on his lap.

When I clattered down the stairs and pushed through the 70s style bead curtain in the doorway that separated store from apartment, Unraveled was empty of customers.

As per usual, one of my directionally challenged curls snagged on a bead strand, giving rise to funky dance moves to avoid being scalped. Finally untangled, I came face to face with the haughty gaze of Nana Dee-Dee's other pride and joy—Pearl.

Tail neatly curled around her paws, she sat on the edge of the service counter, silently judging. Silky black, like her litter brother, Pearl was a lean, mean thieving machine; in perfect contrast to Kit's penchant for gobbling up human food whenever the opportunity arose. I didn't doubt for a second that it had been her who spied the unattended pastry box on a perimeter prowl.

Making the two-fingered *I'm watching you* gesture in her direction, I said, "Don't think I don't know who was behind the stolen pastries, girlfriend."

The cat's eyelids lowered to half-mast as I bored her with my silly prattling. *Human, you are dismissed.*

I rolled my eyes for her, since a cat can't, and flicked over the 'Back in a Tick!' sign that hung on Unraveled's door.

It was a beautiful Discovery summer's day, the sunshine beating down with such vigor I could feel the sidewalk's heat beneath my flip-flop-clad feet. As I passed my retail neighbors—Bloomin' Great Discovery Florists and Chic Threads—I waved a cheery hello. A light sea breeze rolled off the turquoise ocean at the far end of Cape Street, Cape Discovery's main thoroughfare, and I promised myself another early morning swim later this week if the nice weather held.

Spoiler alert: During a Discovery summer, the weather's always nice.

The center of town—which, in all honesty, put the small in 'small town'—consisted of Cape Street, which ran perpendicular to the beach and led to the highly sought-after real estate of more upmarket stores and eateries along the waterfront. Unraveled was not located at the 'highly sought-after real estate' end of town, but at the other, now less-than-desirable part of Discovery.

A sideways glance across the road revealed the source of locals' discomfort. The old butcher shop. Almost eighteen months ago, Nana Dee-Dee and I found the remains of the butcher's wife under it. Although, technically, Kit and Pearl found her.

Well, bits of her.

Sandwiched between the rear concrete wall of a motel and a three-story building that housed a law firm, an accountant, and a dentist's office, the single-story structure had remained empty and boarded up until a month ago. Now it housed a pop-up store selling everything from beach apparel and toys to discounted grocery staples, household goods, cheap books, and party supplies. The inventory went on. And thanks to my younger brother, Sean, being the only employee, I got to hear all about how the new owner had ruffled a few feathers.

I continued along Cape, narrowly avoiding a collision with two kids riding bikes one-handed, their other hands clutching dripping ice cream cones. Disco's sat opposite a small park and kids' playground, on the cross street closest to the center of the town proper. The bakery was packed every morning with parents caffeinating after the school drop-off and busy each lunchtime with locals nipping out for freshly made sourdough sandwiches. Then flat out again in the afternoon as summer tourists and parents vied for outside seats so they could watch their offspring make use of the playground equipment.

I'd missed the lunch crowd, but Disco's was still half-filled with sunscreen and sweaty, smelly customers. From a glance at the display cabinets, I could tell that pastries wouldn't be included in tonight's refreshments. I peered around a sand-speckled family of four to another display cabinet, hoping against hope that there might be a few cinnamon scones or slices of chocolate mud cake left. My hopes were dashed as the two kids pointed at the last remaining scones, and Jules, the mid-twenty-something baker who made me feel like a cougar just by looking at him, slid them into a logo-printed box.

Not that two scones would have fed a dozen ravenous crafters. Unless Harry had some serious loaves-to-fishes miracle tucked up his sleeve.

In despair, I hurried out of Disco's and headed back to Cape Street. Across the road from me stood Discovery's sole grocery store: Hanburys. Perhaps I needed to rethink the cookie option. Because the only other acceptable alternative to pastries from Disco's was to be found at the Daily Grind on the waterfront—a trendy café owned by my high school nemesis, Rosie Cooper.

Big hairy yarn *balls*.

ON ANY VISITS home over the past fifteen years, I'd mostly managed to avoid bumping into Rosie. The approximately thirty seconds of *What've you been up to?* and *You haven't changed a bit!* awkward chitchat that inevitably followed was excruciating. Until one of us beat a hasty retreat, usually with an excuse of the *late for a root canal* variety.

Fortunately, Rosie was surprisingly easy to avoid. For

one, she seemed to spend every waking moment at her café. And two, her family was Cape Discovery's equivalent of royalty—albeit the kind that keeps the tabloids in business. Whereas mine were of more common stock; definitely not the right people to socialize with.

And all the way through high school, Rosie and her cliquey group never let me forget it.

That I'd venture anywhere near the Daily Grind must give you an idea of how desperate I was for tonight's class to be a success. I wanted Harry to enjoy himself, to not give him any reason to retreat into his shell again. Resuming the weekly class was just what he needed to start living again.

So I pulled up my big girl panties and slunk into the café.

The sweet-treats display cabinet still held loads of delicious-looking slices and even three-quarters of a frosted carrot cake. Score! The only thing dampening my enthusiasm currently stood behind the counter in a hot-pink Daily Grind logoed apron. Rosie chatted to a customer while working a giant espresso machine, looking as perfect and cool as the iced coffee she was creating. Nordic blonde hair scraped into a cheerleader's ponytail and black-lashed, chilly blue eyes that narrowed almost imperceptibly when they landed on me.

Me, with my slightly frizzy shoulder-length curls in a color that could kindly be described as dark blonde, or unkindly as *le mouse fur*. And the me dressed in ancient flip-flops and a floral cotton skirt that even Nana Dee-Dee would have called dowdy and refused to wear.

Although I couldn't help but compare Rosie's perfection to my imperfections, I was still comfortable in my skin. Content with my outer packaging while aware there was some room for improvement on the inside. Shouldn't we always strive to be a better person tomorrow than we are today?

With that attitude, I fixed a non-combative smile on my face as Rosie's iced coffee customer collected his go-cup and moved aside. "Hi, Rosie."

Her button nose crinkled as if I were a carton of milk souring in the sun. "What can I get you?"

Guess she wasn't about to invite me to join her in the *Why Did You Really Move Back to Discovery?* quickstep. Others had, but only my family knew why I'd packed up my life and driven five hours south to resume my old one. I was especially good with Rosie not knowing—her with the perfect husband, perfect kids, perfect life.

"I'll take the rest of that carrot cake." I mentally calculated how many 'yes' replies I'd received to the group invite emailed out earlier in the week. "And I'd better have some of those cherry-chocolate slices."

Rosie pursed her lips. "They're *carob*, not chocolate. Vegan and gluten free."

As per the neatly printed sign in front of them. *Doh.* "I don't think anyone will mind as long as they taste good."

Rosie added folded arms to her body language of insulted café owner. "Of course they taste good. Mum baked them fresh this morning."

"Splendid." Who, other than those in the over-sixties age group, says splendid? Obviously, I was spending way too much time with Harry and the predominantly retired patrons of Unraveled. "I'll have a half dozen, thanks."

"Diet blowout, Tessa?"

Oh, so she *did* remember my name.

If not for the reason why I'd ventured into Rosie's lair in

the first place, I would've met snark with snark—I was no longer that scared little mouse hiding in corners.

Harry, I reminded myself. *For Harry*.

"They're for the Crafting for Calmness class tonight."

Rosie cocked her head, ponytail swinging jauntily to one side. "*You're* taking over that?"

The disbelief in her tone needled me harder than her diet comment. "I believe I'm capable of running a weekly class until Harry's up to it again. Anyway, knitting and crochet are great for relaxation and mood boosting. Maybe you should try it."

I'd said more than I'd intended, and I certainly hadn't meant to extend an open invitation to what I'd begun to think of as *my* class.

"My aunt raved about Nana Dee-Dee's weekly get-togethers."

Maybe I imagined it, but Rosie's glacial expression appeared to defrost slightly at my nana's name. Until one of the customers in the line forming behind me oh-so subtly cleared their throat.

Aaaand the permafrost reappeared in Rosie's eyes. "Cake and slice coming up." She snatched up a couple of to-go boxes on her way to the cabinet.

While studiously ignoring her transferring baked goods, I stared at the café's community noticeboard. Too far away to read any of the flyers, I flicked my gaze across the photos submitted for some fundraising competition and listened to snippets of conversations from the surrounding tables.

"...and I reminded her of his outrageous behavior last Wednesday night."

"...of course, my Cydney took top prize..."

"...a Kiwi version of a young George Clooney."

"...spinach, not seaweed. Just try it, sweetie, pretty please?"

"Here." Rosie interrupted my eavesdropping by sliding the two boxes across the counter. She rang them up.

Since there seemed nothing more to say, other than thanks—because I was raised to use my manners regardless of anyone's snotty attitude—I headed to the exit.

Balancing the two boxes, I strode back toward Unraveled, choosing the other side of Cape Street this time to keep the cake and slices in the shade. I'd just reached the far corner of the old butcher shop when the door slammed open, and Ed Hanbury marched out.

If I had to use one word to describe the town's grocery store owner, it would be uptight. From his not-a-strand-out-of-place nineteen-forties gentleman's haircut to his stiff white button-down shirt and polished dress shoes, Ed normally epitomized that word. Today, however, his hair stood in jagged spikes, his tie and shirt collar sat askew, and blotches marred his milk-pale complexion.

As he whirled around in the doorway, Ed didn't see me partially hidden behind an outside display of inflatable beach toys. He smacked his palm against the open door, slamming it into the outer wall and setting the wind chime hooked over the back jingling like Santa's sleigh bowling over a reindeer.

"I'm not the only one in town who wants you gone," Ed shouted into the shop. "Go peddle your imported garbage somewhere else."

I didn't hear the response to Ed's angry outburst because he released the door and gave it a helpful kick on its way closed. His mouth pulling into an exaggerated frown, he straightened and smoothed down his hair, after which he swiped what I assumed was a product-slicked palm down his pants leg. He made a harrumphing sound, which startled me and my right elbow. It jerked sideways, hit a blown-up seahorse, and sent it and a dozen other psychedelic inflatables bouncing to the ground.

Ed whipped his head to the side, catching me gawping over my cake boxes and surrounded by dolphins, orcas, and a ghoulishly grinning shark.

"Hey, Mr. Hanbury."

"Miss Wakefield." His gingery eyebrows arrowed down. "I'm sorry you had to witness that unpleasantness."

"Oh, it's noth—" Something squished beneath my foot with a hiss as I shuffled forward a half step. A bug-eyed mermaid glared up at me.

"Nevertheless, I stand behind my accusation. Lucas Kerr is a"—Ed glared through the store's front window—"is a parasitic leech sucking dry the blood of this town."

Before I could offer my opinion, Ed stomped past me and strode back toward his store. I lifted my foot off the partially deflated mermaid, who was giving me the stink eye, and calculated the odds of reviving her with mouth-to-mouth. Still softly hissing, she was growing skinnier by the second.

Not good then.

"Tess?"

My brother's familiar voice jerked me around. He reached out to steady me as I stumbled, and another innocent sea creature hissed in despair. Luckily, I kept my grip on the café boxes.

"Whoa, now." Sean laughed, and I looked up into his face.

His exceptionally handsome face that, more often than not, got him into trouble with women who should know better. Yes, I'm biased about his outward appeal. Yes, I know he's made some not so savvy decisions over the years. And yes, as the youngest sibling and only boy with three older sisters, he's probably been coddled and excused far too much.

But he was still my baby brother.

"Move out the way before you hurt yourself or drop those boxes," he ordered. "I'll sort this out."

Stepping aside, I angled my head toward Ed's retreating figure. "What was that all about?"

Sean's nose crinkled. "Old Ed ranting at my boss?"

"Yeah. He seemed pretty steamed."

"Eh." Sean shrugged then stooped to collect an armful of inflatables. "He's always got a flea up his butt about something or someone. This month's flavor is Lucas."

I couldn't help myself. "A *bug* up his butt."

A blank look. "Whatever. Some sort of insect." He stacked the squeaky, non-hissing PVC inflatables back on the stand and shot a wary grimace toward the store. "Ed's not all wrong." His voice dropped to a conspirator's level. "There's a rumor going round that Lucas wants to turn this place into a more permanent store. Dad's been hearing grumbles about declining sales and discussions on what can be done through DOPE."

DOPE being the acronym for Discovery's Organization of Professional Entrepreneurs, something Rosie's father, who started it a way back, hadn't considered when naming it. Ed was one of the founding members and the loudest squeaky wheel.

I opened my mouth to ask more, but Sean shook his head with another darting glance. "I've gotta get back to work. Come over first thing tomorrow morning before I open up. I'm on the first shift alone. I need your sisterly advice on something." He gave me a wonky smile—one which could turn the knees of half of Cape Discovery's female population to jelly—and disappeared inside.

Shivery spider legs scurried down my spine as I crossed the road. Out of all my siblings, Sean was the one least likely to ask anyone for advice. That he had was tantamount to the four horsemen of the apocalypse riding into town.

TWO

That evening, Beth Chadwick was the first to arrive at Unraveled. A sixty-something widow and longtime regular customer, she waddled into the workroom like she owned majority shares in the business. After casting her beady-eyed stare around, she examined the food set out on the worktable that dominated the room, then sniffed her approval. She chose a seat near Harry, who sat at the far end of the rectangular table. It was a badly kept secret that Beth had a teeny crush on my granddad.

Right behind Beth came Mary and Gerald Hopkins, perhaps the cutest elderly couple ever. After my grandparents, of course. Another longtimer, Mary was the founding rebel crocheter, who insisted that she and three other ladies be called the Happy Hookers. Thus differentiating them from the knitters, who jokingly referred to themselves as the Serial Knitters. Believe me, there was much heated discussion and controversy among the group over that! I suspected poor Gerald only tagged along for the cake and company. And because he clearly adored his feisty wife.

Next, in quick succession, arrived three of the groups'

younger members. There was Skye Johnson, a new-to-town hairstylist, whose multi-colored streaked locks and Doc Martens combat boots shot the older ladies' gray eyebrows up to their equally gray hair. Isabel Burton, Cape Discovery High School's principal, who couldn't have pets due to allergies so had to satisfy herself with keeping treats in her bag for Kit and Pearl. And lastly, Haley Cole, heavily pregnant with her first child and knitting baby hats and booties as if she expected the kid to have six plus heads and ten feet.

Fifteen minutes after everyone had unpacked their current project and sat down with their hot drink of choice, Pamela Martin, owner of Chic Threads clothing boutique, made her grand entrance. Sweeping in on a gust of cooler evening air, she swirled around the room to air-kiss everyone, leaving a wash of cloying perfume in her wake. Pamela was Rosie Cooper's aunt, and, if pressed to make a choice, I'd rather be stuck in a room with my old nemesis. At least Rosie made no bones about disliking me—although, strangely enough, she'd added a half dozen extra slices to the to-go boxes free of charge.

Pamela was more of an expert in passive-aggressive warfare. And while I didn't think she loathed me, I certainly wasn't on speed-dial if she needed a cappuccino pal.

"Dreadfully sorry I'm late," she announced as if we'd all been on tenterhooks waiting for her to make an appearance. "But I stopped to chat with the pop-up store's proprietor. He's a most charming, urbane man. Gracious"—she fanned her face dramatically—"I'm all discombobulated."

She plopped into a spare seat and turned to Haley, who sat next to her. "Darling, would you get me a cup of tea? I'm parched after all that scintillating conversation."

Before Haley could maneuver her baby belly out from under the table, I leaped to my feet. "I'll get it, Pam."

Pamela slitted her thickly-coated-with-mascara lashes at me. "It's *Pamela*, darling. Pam sounds so dreadfully common."

I glanced over at the corner of the room, where an electric kettle and a selection of mugs, tea bags, and a fragrant pot of coffee sat on the counter, next to the sink. "Sorry, Pam*ela*. English breakfast or Earl Grey?"

Her nose crinkled. "Dee-Dee always had green tea with lemon tea bags set aside for me. Do you have any of those?"

"They're upstairs in the pantry," Harry said. "I can fetch them for you."

"No, I'll do it. You'll lose your place if you put down your needles." I dipped my chin to the complicated Fair Isle beanie he was knitting—a hat Nana Dee-Dee hadn't had time to complete.

As I walked toward the door, Skye rolled her eyes at me in silent solidarity, and Mary whispered something in her husband's ear that had him clicking his tongue in agreement.

"Oh, and Tessa?" Pamela called from her seat as I reached the open doorway between craft room and store. "On the return trip, can you fetch me a couple more balls of that delicious magenta yarn I bought the other day? You know, the possum-merino blend. Just put it on my tab."

Have I mentioned Pamela's a yarn snob? Fortunately, her expensive taste in yarns and tendency to hoard them was one of the reasons my grandparents had stayed in business.

"Sure."

I slipped through the brightly lit store and trailed my fingertips up the worn banister as I climbed the stairs. The cozy apartment felt more like home than my own family home. As a kid, I'd spent many hours with my grandparents, whereas my older sisters preferred socializing with their peers, and my brother was busy with after-school rugby training. While Harry worked at Cape Discovery's small police station, I dropped stitches and eventually knitted wonky scarves under Nana Dee-Dee's patient tutelage.

Tears prickled the corners of my eyes as I pushed open the kitchen door and crossed to the pantry. "Miss you so much, Nana."

A soft mew at my ankle jerked my gaze down. Pearl stared up at me with an unnerving focus that had me convinced she understood my lame human emotions.

"Guess you're after a treat." With a sniff, I reached down to tickle between her pointy ears—often the only safe spot to touch on her lithe body.

Pearl rose on her hind legs and bunted my palm then rested her front paws on my legs. All the while keeping her razor-sharp claws sheathed. She tapped her soft pads against my bare skin and mewed again, arching her spine.

Huh. Anyone who didn't know her better would think she wanted to be picked up and...cuddled? Against my better judgment, I scooped her up, and she snuggled into the crook of my neck, purring into my ear.

"You miss her too, don't you?" Tears spilled down my cheeks and rolled off my jaw, a couple of them plopping wetly onto her fur.

Pearl's purring ceased, and she reared back to give me the evil eye for daring to let anything wet touch her body. Then, with a whisker twitch, she hauled herself up, up until she'd draped herself around my neck like a fur stole.

Once comfortable, she resumed her purring.

I froze, too stunned—and maybe a fraction terrified—to move. The only person Pearl sat on like this was Nana Dee-Dee. *The only person. Ever.*

Until tonight.

And for some weird 'woo-woo' reason, I felt Nana Dee-Dee nearby...and that my nana had passed her love, and yes, some responsibility, onto my shoulders.

After finding the green tea at the back of the pantry, I crouched to countertop height and tentatively tickled under Pearl's chin. "Pamela's here tonight, so you'd better stay in the apartment."

Claws flexing on my shoulder, Pearl stood then jumped onto the counter, her tail flicking from side to side as she strolled away.

"Sensible choice."

Pamela was one of those people who didn't get that cats chose whether they wanted to interact with you, not the other way around.

Dabbing my tear-damp eyes with a tissue, I headed back downstairs. After noting the extra yarn on a scrap of paper to add to Pamela's account—which, along with the rest of Unraveled's admin, I'd taken it upon myself to shift into the digital age—I selected two balls from the shelf and returned to the workroom.

Fortunately, Pamela's needles were a clicking blur as she chatted to Haley about her brother's new baby, and how scandalous it was to have a child at his age, but nevertheless, these things happen. Quietly setting the yarn by her elbow, not wanting to draw her attention to my bloodshot eyes, I kept my gaze down. As I prepared Pamela's drink, I listened to the soothing clicks and rustles of crafting with half an ear but was unable to ignore the conversation between Skye and Mary, who were positioned closest to me.

"...went in for some of that caramel popcorn, even though it sticks to Gerald's dentures, and came out with scented candles, a new set of steak knives, and even a few balls of cheap and cheerful acrylic." Mary shot me an apologetic glance. "Sorry, Tessa, but it was less than two dollars a ball, and it'll be perfect for making next year's Christmas decorations."

Less than two dollars a ball?

We couldn't possibly compete with those prices, even with the few synthetic yarns we stocked. Nana Dee-Dee had believed in supporting local spinners and dyers, who used natural fibers such as wool and alpaca, and blends with silk, cotton, and bamboo. We supplied other branded yarns to remain competitive, but our suppliers understood Unraveled's loyalties would always lie with locals.

However, Mary looked so worried that I pushed my concerns aside. "Don't be silly, Mary. Of course you had to grab a bargain when you saw one."

Her gnarled fingers relaxed around her crochet hook. "He was very persuasive, I must say."

"Who? Sean?" Skye, working on a slightly wonky-sided scarf that Mary was teaching her to crochet, bounced upright in her chair.

I mentally sighed at the way her eyes lit up.

"Gracious, no." Mary chuckled and pointed a finger at the extra chain in the pattern that Skye had forgotten to add. "I meant the owner, Lucas. He's quite dashing. Like a young Cary Grant."

Skye poked out her tongue, the silver stud in it catching the light. "If you're into that whole used-car-salesman vibe. The man's a creeper."

Isabel glanced up from the shawl she was knitting, spots of color pinking her cheeks. "Has he done or said something inappropriate to you?"

"Nah. Nothing like that." Skye repositioned the yarn around the fingers of her left hand. "I guess he might be okay once you get to know him. Like the new English teacher at your school. My sister thought he was stuck-up at first, but he's just a little shy."

"Oh, is that Sven Andrews?" Haley said. "The Star Wars superfan?"

"That's him."

The conversation then veered off into favorite teachers and the use of pop culture in high school classes. Once I'd finished brewing the green tea, I carried the mug over to Pamela and picked up a cherry and *carob* slice for myself. As I returned to my seat at the table, I took a bite.

Although I hated to admit it, Rosie gave good slice.

And while I successfully commanded my brain not to worry over how many calories were in carob versus chocolate, I couldn't stop it from wondering if the pop-up store's cheap and cheerful yarn was the reason Unraveled's January sales had been a lot slower than usual.

I made a mental note to ask Sean about it tomorrow.

THE NEXT MORNING, I was up with the birds. Or, to be more precise, the yowling of cats and the tweeting, wild fluttering death throes of a bird. As Armageddon could arrive with the dawn and my granddad would still sleep through until precisely seven thirty, when his alarm clock beeped, I crawled out of bed to see what Pearl had dragged in through the cat door downstairs. Before the cats spread bird guts and feathers all through Unraveled.

It wouldn't be the first or the last time I mopped up blood from a feline crime scene.

Wrapped in my robe, I fetched a dustpan and broom and trudged down the stairs. Both cats sat in the entranceway beside the back door, tails curled around their paws, looking like a pair of fun-sized gargoyles. One of said gargoyles appeared immensely proud of herself.

"*Purrrt,*" said Pearl.

I'd almost place a bet she was the murderer, though Kit was the one with the downy feather clinging to one ear. Apparently, cats brought their humans prey because they regarded us as big, dumb kittens who couldn't hunt for ourselves. Noting their smug but curious expressions as they watched me scoop up the poor birdy's corpse, I had to concede the experts were likely correct.

"Good hunting, guys." Could cats' sensitive ears detect sarcasm? "Why don't I put your generous gift outside and fill your food bowls?"

The cats raced upstairs while I dumped the feathered body in the trash and calculated how much coffee I'd need to forget this gruesome start to another Cape Discovery day.

After coffee, cereal, and sleepy conversation with Harry (in that order), I made sure he ate his *breakfast of champions* chocolate spread on toast. I stole a piece to eat on the way to the old butcher shop.

It was early, too early for many tourists to be out and about, but still plenty of locals indulging in their morning coffee before work. While some cafés catered to the breakfast crowd, most of Discovery's stores and small businesses didn't open until nine. The pop-up store, which opened at eight, being an exception. Lucas Kerr must subscribe to the 'early bird catches the worm' philosophy.

As I crossed the road, licking the last trace of melted chocolate off my thumb, I spotted the closed sign hanging on the store's door. I checked my watch: seven thirty-five. Sean would have arrived five minutes ago. Under normal circumstances, I wouldn't have a clue about my brother's routine. But since he'd started working at the pop-up store a couple of months ago, I'd had to suffer through a litany of complaints about early morning starts during family dinners.

I knocked, expecting Sean to bounce up between the rows of shelves. But the store remained silent. Dust motes swirled inside, sunshine flaring off the windows where pork chops and sausages had once been displayed. Perhaps he was out in the back room, headphones clamped to his ears, blissfully unaware I'd arrived. Pointlessly, I glanced at my watch again. Sean wasn't the only one who had to work this morning, not that he was known for considering other people's needs.

When I tried the door, I assumed it'd still be locked, but it wasn't. I jumped back a step as it swung outward toward my nose. *Whew—close call*. Poking my head through the open doorway, turtle-style, I called my brother's name.

Once...and then again. More silence.

Skin tightened across my forehead as I frowned. "Don't tell me you forgot to lock up last night, Sean."

I hovered in the doorway, uncertain of the best course of action. Nothing in the store appeared out of place. Petty thieves hadn't taken advantage of the unlocked door to raid packets of imported candy or pilfer baseball caps. I could just flick the old-fashioned lock and shut the door—no one would be any the wiser...

Something brushed against my bare calf, and I let out a high-pitched sound that probably only the neighborhood dogs' sensitive ears would have heard. I glanced down and saw twin tails flying high as two black cats trotted into the store.

"Kit! Pearl! Get back here," I hissed as they sauntered along the center aisle.

Blasting telepathic insults at the pair, I slipped inside and closed the door behind me. This wasn't the first time the cats had followed me, and perhaps the sly little devils remembered this used to be a butcher shop. They were in for a rude surprise if they expected to find an unattended pork chop on one of the shelves. I hurried past a display of greeting cards, packaged candy, and kitchen utensils. Meanwhile, Kit and Pearl had vanished behind the service counter.

Shivering sheep sherbet.

The door between the storefront and the back room that the butcher had used to, uh, *prepare his goods* was cracked open. And I'd bet a dozen cherry and carob slices the cats would sneak through it.

Any cat that could resist an open door wasn't much of a cat.

This worked to my advantage. It was easier to corral two nosy felines in a small room with few hiding spots than it would be among shelves and the hundreds of items they could knock off them. Sure enough, when I rounded the counter, I spotted the tip of a tail disappearing through the gap.

Then one of the cats let out a yowl unlike any I'd ever heard before. The eeriness of the low, echoing sound swept a prickling across my scalp and down my spine. Swear I've never been the superstitious sort, but at that moment, I wished for a handful of salt to toss over my shoulder. Or maybe a garlic necklace and a silver bullet because my instincts were screaming vampire-werewolf-ghost-of-a-butcher's-wife.

I admit I hesitated, my bare toes curling on my rubber flip-flops, ready to bolt back the way I came and let Sean deal with the fallout of my cats.

Or rather, *Nana Dee-Dee's* cats.

Another gut-twisting growly yowl came from behind the door.

Whether Nana Dee-Dee's cats or mine, I couldn't desert them when they were clearly upset about something. I was being ridiculous. With a last glance over my shoulder to see if Sean had arrived—he hadn't—I pushed open the door and barged inside.

Nothing much had changed from the last time I was in this room. L-shaped work surfaces still ran along the walls, although they were now covered with boxes of stock, and the large island counter took up most of the available floor space. An unpleasant metallic smell hung in the air, taking me straight back to when the butcher shop still had carcasses stored in the walk-in chiller and knives lying around on blood-soaked chopping blocks.

And let's not mention the body buried in the crawl space under the floor.

But one thing differed dramatically from that time.

A boat-shoe-clad foot lay on the floor, sticking out from behind the island counter.

THREE

I CLAMPED a hand over my shocked yelp, not wanting to be one of those women who shrieked then regressed to hand wringing while exclaiming, "Oh, the *horror.*"

Breathing through my nose, sounding much like a hyperventilating Darth Vader, I blinked down at the expensive-looking boat shoe and the foot inside. A band of reddened, hairless skin encircled the ankle. It looked as if someone had treated him to a bad leg wax.

But the foot definitely wasn't Sean's; this thought struck me with instant relief. The last time my brother fitted a shoe that small was when he was twelve. Plus, he wouldn't be seen dead in boat shoes.

Dead. In. Boat. Shoes.

I shuddered but finally managed to peel my hand away from my mouth and take a—relatively—normal breath.

"Excuse me? Hello? Are you okay...?" My heart rate tripling, I waited for the shoe to move.

Because, you know, Boat-Shoe-Guy must have passed out from the world's worst paper cut; the only injury I was willing to believe might explain the crimson splatters speckling the floor. He was sure to come around... any...second...now.

Nope. Still no movement.

My gaze zipped from the floor to Kit. His whiskers quivering, he stood near the corner of the workbench, back rounded in a witch's cat arch. From somewhere behind the bench came a light clinking sound. I hoped Pearl wasn't emptying the poor man's pockets. The little thief.

But even if Pearl was committing larceny, I couldn't put off the inevitable for one panicked heartbeat longer. Squeezing my eyelids into visually narrowed blinkers and giving the workbench a wide berth, I sucked in oxygen, held it, and glanced down at Boat-Shoe-Guy.

And yup. I now had to change his nickname to *Dead*-Boat-Shoe-Guy.

Protective squinting and complete lack of medical training aside, it was obvious even to me that Elvis had well and truly left the building. Or in this case, as the dearly departed wasn't sporting a sparkly jumpsuit or pompadour hairstyle, the store owner, Lucas Kerr.

He lay sprawled on his stomach, his sightless gaze directed at the back door and the two-seater couch beside it. If the bloodied head wound wasn't sufficient evidence that the man was on the wrong side of living, then the chef's knife sticking out of his back was a clincher.

Pinned by the knife was a piece of paper printed with wobbly capitals: YOU WERE TOLD TO GET OUT OF TOWN!

So, not only was Lucas Kerr Dead-Boat-Shoe-Guy, but he was also *Murdered*-Dead-Boat-Shoe-Guy.

Out of the corner of my eye, I spotted Pearl close to a small staff refrigerator. She was playing with something she'd found, batting it with her paw and then pouncing.

Clearly traumatized by the nearby dead body. She flicked the object into the air, and I saw it was small and metallic.

I hurried over and snatched it up. It was a Saint Patrick's Day pin, complete with a rosy-cheeked leprechaun waving a four-leafed clover. As I glanced around at the boxes of stock to see if it'd fallen from one, the squeak of the door opening made me jump. Instinctively, I dropped the badge into my pocket.

"Tessa?"

My gaze shot to Sean, who stood in the doorway, gawking in the direction of Lucas's foot. He raked his fingers through his already rumpled hair and stepped inside, the door swinging shut behind him.

"What are you...who is...is that my boss?" Without waiting for an answer, Sean strode to the workbench, stuttering to a halt as he stared down at Lucas's body. "What the...?"

A black shadow appeared by his ankles, but before I could shout a warning, Kit twined around them. My brother let out a scream worthy of a Bela Lugosi movie heroine as, arms windmilling, he stumbled backward. His flailing would have been hilarious in any other situation, not so much in this one. By the time he'd gotten control of his gangly limbs, Pearl and Kit had retreated to the far corner of the room.

"You brought Nana's cats in here, Tess?"

"No. Jeez. No. They must've followed me, and when I opened the door, they ran inside and..." I shudderingly ran out of air. At this rate, I'd need to hyperventilate into one of those non-eco-friendly plastic bags stacked in a pile. But would plastic still work?

With a huff somewhere between impatience and panic, Sean strode over and grabbed my arm. He towed me around to the other side of the workbench, away from his boss's body. "The door was unlocked?" he asked.

"I thought you must already be inside."

"Yeah, hit snooze one too many times and got up late." He gave me an awkward half-hug around the shoulders. "You okay?"

"Not my first dead body." I'd aimed for nonchalance, but the quaver in my voice probably gave me away.

"A finger bone doesn't count." One last half-hug, then Sean pulled out his phone. "Wait over there while I call the cops."

He turned away, and I drifted over to the cats, who were still grooming themselves in the corner while keeping a careful eye on things.

Above the cats was a counter, sink, kettle, and cups for making tea and coffee. As I reached for a cup, planning to pour myself a drink of water, I spotted a used one by the sink. With a trace of lipstick on the rim, it contained the dregs of what looked like raspberry tea.

I bent and sniffed. Not tea, some kind of...red wine? Having watched enough crime shows with Harry and been regaled with stories from his days on the force, I knew not to touch. Didn't stop me examining the dried red ring staining the countertop where another cup must have sat though.

As the clipped sounds of my brother's phone conversation continued in the background, I couldn't help but imagine a brief timeline.

Sean didn't lock up every night, and even if he did, he'd told me Lucas sometimes came back later in the evening to catch up on paperwork. Was that what he'd done last night? Drunk red wine on his couch while he worked?

Or maybe he'd arranged for a rendezvous that required a

greater degree of privacy than his motorhome parked in the local campground afforded. According to brotherly gossip, Lucas paid the owners double the normal rate to park his vehicle in the far corner of the campground. Away from those who might wish to spy on his comings and goings—or his female visitors' comings and goings. Of course, there was only so much privacy one could reasonably expect in a small town.

I remembered the note. Meeting someone here after hours didn't necessarily mean a romantic tryst. Lucas Kerr hadn't been a popular man, but he might have agreed to discuss business with a rival over a drink.

Or the shared wine resulting in a lipstick-smeared cup might have occurred before the killer's arrival.

Or a crafty murderer might have smeared lipstick on the rim to direct suspicion away from their gender.

Or, or, or...

I reined in the thoughts swirling around in my head. *Observe the facts, Tessa.*

Right.

From where I stood, I could see the back door's lock was still engaged. Unless Lucas had accidentally or deliberately left the shop door open and someone had entered that way, the only other option was he'd let the killer in through the back door.

And then they'd tied him up and stabbed him with a handy chef's knife from his stock?

Another peek at Lucas.

He wore trendy khaki shorts and a white shirt. Blood splatter had dried on the shirt sleeves, but there was little around the knife. With a wince, I skimmed my gaze upward again to the man's face and over the nasty wound on his temple. The source of most of the blood.

My stomach lurched, threatening to evict the chocolate toast.

I bent and scooped up Kit, the feline less likely to contaminate the crime scene further by shredding me with their claws. Figuring Pearl would follow her brother as she usually did, I glanced down at my foot. I'd heard slurpy grooming sounds coming from her only a moment ago, but once again, she'd disappeared.

I side-eyed Sean, still with his phone to his ear, his smiling three-quarter profile telling me there was a female operator on the line. Good. While he was distracted, I had time to herd both cats outside before they could do any damage. Since Pearl couldn't have ghosted through a closed door into the main shop, there was only one other place she could be.

Keeping a tight grip on Kit, who rested his front paws on my shoulder and seemed quite content looking around from that vantage point, I edged over to what had once been the walk-in chiller. The door stood ajar, and mindful of fingerprints, I used my elbow to push it further open.

The hanging carcass hooks had been removed, and metal shelving now lined the walls. These shelves were crammed with more cardboard boxes, many of them ripped open, their contents spilling onto the floor.

Ransacked was the word that sprang to mind. Someone —possibly the killer—must have ransacked the storeroom.

Looking for what?

PERCHED on an upturned cardboard box amid the chaos, Pearl stared intently up at a high shelf overflowing with a jumble of torn-open packaging. I moved closer, trying to see what she was seeing. But before I could, she leaped nimbly onto the shelf and sniffed around.

"Pearl," I whispered, "get down from there."

Naturally, she ignored me. Forced farther into the room, with Kit purring like a lawnmower in my ear, I was now close enough to spot the object of her fascination. A ceramic cat figurine with one raised paw. A Japanese lucky cat, or whatever they were officially called.

She curled a paw around its base and hooked it toward her—and the shelf edge. You can see where I'm going with this, right?

"Stop that right now."

With the sixth, seventh, or eighth extra sense cats seem to possess, Kit switched his focus from purring to the fun his sister was having without him. He arched away from me, trying to join her. Grappling with the furry, clawed, octopus-like creature determined to escape my grasp meant I foresaw the not-so-lucky ceramic cat's demise but was helpless to prevent it.

"Don't. You. Dare."

She dared.

Pearl nudged the figurine again, paused to check she had my undivided attention, then tipped the lucky cat off the shelf. Gravity took over, and it plummeted, shattering on impact behind an upturned box.

Sean appeared in the doorway. "What was that?" He spotted Pearl. "Are you nuts? The cops'll be here any minute. Get her down from there."

I peeled Kit off my shoulder, along with a fair amount of skin evidence caught in his claws, and held him out to my brother. "Take him. I can't get her down with one arm."

Kit flattened his ears at Sean, who wore the same

expression as a man asked to handle a cobra. "Uh. He looks annoyed. Is he going to bite?"

"Probably. But you weigh eighty kilos, and he's only five. You do the math." I pushed the tail-twitching Kit into Sean's chest. With a resigned sigh, he smushed one hand on the cat's shoulders and the other just above his tail.

This wouldn't end well.

"Take him out the front and let him go," I said. "I'll be out with her in a minute, and they'll make their own way home."

Sean backed out of the storeroom as if he were handling an explosive device. Which, to be fair, he kind of was.

I made kissy noises in Pearl's direction as I eased between boxes, trying not to crush anything beneath my feet. Behind the upturned box lay shards of Lucky Cat, a corner of a plastic baggie peeking out from underneath one large piece.

Curiosity overturning caution, I bent down to flick over the shard. Taped to the inside was a matchbox-sized plastic baggie filled with...pills. Air whooshed out of me, and I froze, palms braced on my thighs.

Were those what I thought they were?

Still hunched over, I was alerted to another's presence by the heavy tread of footsteps. I glanced sideways to see Jeremy Austin, one of Cape Discovery's constables, standing in the doorway, thumbs hooked into his stab-proof vest. *Poor Lucas Kerr might've gotten more use out of that,* I couldn't help but think.

"Ms. Wakefield?"

Swap Officer Austin's boring blue uniform for a wetsuit, and you couldn't pick him out of a lineup of middle-aged surfer stereotypes. The few times I'd spoken to him since returning home, I'd kept expecting him to call me 'dude.'

So far, he hadn't.

Giving him a little wave of acknowledgment, I went to straighten, but Pearl chose that exact moment to leap down from the shelf. She used me as a convenient stepladder, launching herself off my back, claws dug in for good measure. Nice. I uncurled with a grimace, hoping I wouldn't contaminate the crime scene further by bleeding from eight parallel scratches across my spine. Guess that's what a crazy cat lady gets instead of a tramp-stamp on her lower back.

Officer Austin stared down his nose at Pearl, who was butting up against his legs, tail flirtatiously twisting around them. "Ms. Wakefield, is this your cat?"

She was such a suck-up.

"Technically, she's my nana's cat." I zigzagged toward him through the boxes.

"Let me rephrase that. Why is there a cat in here?" He took a backward step away from said cat, perhaps trying to avoid a furry coating on his uniform pants.

Good luck with that, sir.

"Pearl followed me inside. She does that sometimes because she's incredibly nosy." I shook my head to clear it—there were more important things to discuss with Officer Austin than Pearl's quirky habits. "She hasn't touched anything." Anything being the body out there, getting more and more dead by the second. "Except for an ornament she knocked off the shelf behind me. You might want to take a look at what's inside."

With his height advantage, he only had to take a few steps into the storeroom and lean forward in order to see the little baggie.

"Is it drugs?" I prompted when he frowned but remained silent.

"We'll let the experts decide that, shall we?" he said calmly. As if it were an everyday occurrence to find a baggie of pills in a ransacked storeroom with a knifed owner next door.

"A detective's on his way from Napier. He'll take over. In the meantime, please take the cat and wait outside with your brother."

I dutifully, but warily picked up Pearl. She gazed at the frowning man with a holstered baton, pepper spray, and Taser and went limp in my arms, clearly deciding to behave. Officer Austin moved aside so I could squeeze past. Fortunately, his breadth prevented me from gaining one last look at Lucas Kerr as he escorted me to the front of the shop.

Questions whizzed in circles around my brain, and unable to help myself, I turned back. "Do you think someone killed him for those pills?"

"That's the detective's job to determine, Ms. Wakefield."

I'd been dismissed, and as I suddenly couldn't wait to breathe fresh air, I nodded politely and stepped outside.

As soon as my feet hit the sidewalk, Pearl launched herself off me. She fled in the direction of home, most likely to indulge in an emergency snacking session.

Sean sat on the sidewalk, leaning back against the store as he palmed a handful of potato chips into his mouth. Despite the fact he was disgustingly chewing with his mouth open, I opted to sit near him. Actually, quite close to him. Sure, he was my gross man-child of a brother, but I loved him anyway. And having escaped that claustrophobic storeroom, I could now admit to myself how truly shaken I was.

I stole a chip. Just the one to help calm my nerves.

"You good?" he asked.

With a snort, I stole another. "Peachy." I leaned my head back against the wall then rolled it sideways to give Sean a big sister smackdown stare. "So, where were you last night?"

His eyebrows rose, but he continued to crunch a moment longer. "You're asking for my alibi? Seriously?"

I pulled the facial equivalent of a shrug. "Cops'll be asking you soon as they get here. Might as well practice on someone who knows you're innocent."

"I was at home."

"Doing?"

"Doing a crossword and knitting a doily. Pete's sake, Tess—I was home, reheating one of Mum's care-package casseroles for dinner and eating it in front of the TV. Then I went to bed."

"Can anyone confirm this?"

"You mean, was there someone else in my bed?" He glared back at me. "No. I happen to be taking a break from the onerous task of sleeping with every female in town."

As I went to steal another chip, he yanked the bag out of my reach. Brat—he knew BBQ was my second-favorite potato chip flavor.

"So there's no one who can prove you were home all night?" I pretended I wasn't reaching for the bag and scratched my thigh instead.

Sean sighed. "Sorry, *Miss Fisher*, had I known I'd need someone to vouch for my all-night presence and stamina, I would've invited that new hairstylist for a sleepover."

"You're a pig."

He grinned and offered me the chips. A pig, but at least he was *my* pig.

Around us, people had begun to notice Officer Austin's marked police vehicle parked outside the store. A few bolder locals wandered over to ask what was going on. I kept my gaze locked onto my phone screen, feigning sudden interest in social media posts of funny cat memes and updates on the mundane things people did on a beautiful summer's morning.

One of Sean's talents was people skills, which he successfully employed to evade any direct questions about what was going on inside. As the youngest, he'd learned from his older siblings how to circumvent Mum and Dad's rules and the consequences of breaking them: with charm and misdirection.

However, by the time two more police cars cruised down Cape Street toward us, even Sean's cheeky banter couldn't keep the curious onlookers at bay. Quite a few people now milled around outside the store, and the lead vehicle had to double-park next to a ute and order its driver to move along. As uniformed officers poured onto the sidewalk and immediately began issuing instructions, I caught a glimpse of one man in the second car. He remained in place until the crowd had been ushered aside.

Then, and only then, did he unfold his sizable bulk from the car. And by bulk, I mean six foot something of broad-shouldered, rugby-player-thighed, hands-that-could-crush-a-fistful-of-unshelled-walnuts big. He cut an imposing figure in his charcoal-colored suit, totally out of place in this small seaside town where tidy-casual was considered business attire.

With precision-cut black hair, dark shades, and what might have been a sexy mouth if it wasn't curved downward in a scowl, he strode toward us, his long legs eating up the sidewalk. I didn't need to see behind those shades to know he was sizing up my brother and me because he immediately struck me as a *size 'em up* kind of guy.

He stopped in front of us, arms folded across his chest. "Good morning. I'm Detective Sergeant Mana."

His voice was as deep as a gravel pit and equally as abrasive.

"Hey," Sean said.

I kept my lips zipped. Did he expect a polite greeting in return or an impressed gasp in recognition of his authority?

His gaze slowly swept from Sean's face to mine. "Tell me. Which one of you brought a cat to a crime scene?"

FOUR

I didn't make it back to Unraveled until the early afternoon, and by then, my head throbbed like I'd been at a heavy metal concert. Although I'd swallowed several cups of cheap-and-nasty brewed tea, my throat still felt tender after giving my statement regarding this morning's events to an officer at Cape Discovery's small police station. I couldn't remember specific details of the interview, only that I'd felt like a rundown battery-powered monkey by the end. And I got the impression that the officer typing up my statement had already formed an opinion on our guilt or innocence.

The chilly detective man was still interviewing Sean when I was finally allowed to leave. I debated hanging around, but all I wanted was to get home, shower this morning's events from my skin, and then curl up in my fluffy robe and watch reruns of *Project Runway* with my granddad.

I'd texted my mum and Harry earlier to let them know what was happening, but of course, news spreads like a virus in a small town. With no one spreading it faster than my mother.

And Lucas Kerr's murder would be the number one topic of speculation.

The closed sign hung in Unraveled's front door, so I bypassed it and walked around the corner of the building to the chain-link gate that led into our fenced backyard. Pearl lay stretched out on the edge of a planter box of herbs, dozing in a strip of afternoon sunshine without a care in the world.

Oh, to be a cat.

But some of the tension in my shoulders softened as I ran my hand across the lavender growing in a terracotta pot near the back door. Sniffing my fragrant fingers, I willed Nana Dee-Dee's favorite flower to soothe me with its familiar scent. I slipped inside and was halfway up the stairs when I heard voices other than Harry's drifting down from the apartment. Stopping so fast I nearly fell up the next step, I gripped the handrail and played Statues.

"Sean, baby, is that you?" My mum's voice broke the sudden silence above.

Guess I needed to work on my silent-assassin skills. "No. It's me."

"Oh. Tessa." Two words into which she managed to squeeze a lifetime of loving disapproval.

A long, hot shower and downtime now out of the question, I trudged up the stairs. Mum stood in the kitchen, still in her real estate agent shirt and a dark gray skirt that triggered a flashback of Detective Mana's tailored suit.

She enfolded me in a perfume-choking hug for a full five seconds longer than her standard three. After briskly rubbing my back, she pulled away to give me a maternal once-over and resisted smoothing the curls on one side of my face. All the while, remaining silent.

Wow, who was this woman, and what had she done with my mother?

"How's my baby? Do you think he's okay? Have you seen him?"

Ah, there she was!

I schooled my face into a serious, not-at-all-offended expression while forcibly keeping my eyes from rolling back in my head. "The police interviewed us separately, so I haven't seen him. But he's fine, Mum." And at thirty-two, old enough to not be anyone's baby. "We're *both* fine."

Mum blinked rapidly; I could almost hear her mind whirring. "Well, of course *you* are. You take after Harry and your dad—pragmatists. Nothing fazes you lot. But Sean takes after me. We're more sensitive."

"Highly strung, you mean." My dad wandered into the kitchen, a pair of mugs in his hand and thick wooly socks on his feet. He too must have come straight from work, as he wore his work uniform of grubby coveralls. If I hadn't been so distracted, I would have noticed his well-worn work boots sitting at the back door.

"Alan, please," Mum said as he set the mugs on the counter before wrapping his arms around me.

As Dad squeezed me tight, I smelled traces of well-fertilized earth, fragrant herbs, and a whiff of crushed rose petals on his coveralls. His cottage industry of growing and providing fresh herbs and flowers to businesses in town and the nearest city, Napier, was his pride and joy. After his family, of course.

"All right, then?" he asked, resting his chin on top of my head.

Dad didn't say much. Didn't need to with Mum more than willing to take up any conversational slack. But when he did talk, people listened. His honest warmth had earned him and his business enough loyal customers that he'd been able to employ full-time help for the past two years. Typically for him, he insisted on continuing with deliveries and a lot of the hands-on work in his gardens. But now he could put some eager young muscle to work on the more physical tasks.

"Hunky-dory," I said.

"You will be after a shower and a bite to eat." He released me and angled himself toward the oven. "Scones should be ready soon, and I picked up some cream from Hanburys."

As I peeked past Dad to check Mum wasn't close by, he chuckled—softly. "It's okay. Harry made them."

Finding a smile for him, I tapped the side of my nose and left him to rinse out the mugs.

Once showered and dressed in clean clothes, I felt a little more human and a lot less cyborg. I skipped drying my hair in favor of scoring a scone slathered with butter, jam, and cream.

Darn it, I'd earned that buttery goodness.

But while I'd been busy sloughing off dead-body cooties with super-hot water, Sean had arrived. Mum had settled him in Nana Dee-Dee's La-Z-Boy—now my usual spot—and was handing him a scone with so much whipped cream there was no practical way for my brother to eat it without ending up covered in the stuff.

As I took a seat next to Dad on the couch, Mum perched on the arm beside him, no doubt figuring her skirt wouldn't pick up as many cat hairs there as it would on the cushions. Mum was definitely not a cat person. We all sat there in silence, watching Sean lick cream off his scone.

"So... How did it go?" I asked.

Mum shot me a look—the same one she'd given me when, as a kid, I'd asked a friend of hers why she had blue gunk smeared around her eyes. Sean didn't look up from his whipped-cream removal.

"What?" I mouthed at Dad.

He rubbed a calloused finger along his eyebrow and grimaced.

"He's had a tough time of it, haven't you, my baby?" Mum said.

Sean nodded, cream dotting the tip of his nose.

My mouth settled into a frown. "Really? You found it tough telling the detective you'd come into work and found your boss on the floor with me and two cats standing over him?"

I tried to catch my brother's eye, but for some reason, he refused to look at me.

"Sarcasm is not helpful, Tessa."

Leaning forward, I was close enough to poke Sean's arm. Which I did. Hard. "What's going on? Did Jeremy and Detective Mana play good cop, bad cop a little too enthusiastically?"

Sean finally met my gaze, but only for a second before his eyes flicked to Mum and Dad. "I think I screwed up."

How could you screw up a statement to the police, unless you lied, and then got so tangled up in those lies you inadvertently hogtied yourself? But Sean had nothing to lie about... Did he?

"Spit it out, lad." Harry licked jam off his fingers and picked up the TV remote. "We haven't got all day. *Home and Away* starts soon."

My brother sighed and set down his plate, leaving the other half of his scone untouched. What a waste. "I answered the detective's questions truthfully," he said. "But I didn't mention that I owed Lucas a bit of money."

"A *bit* of money?" Dad repeated with a frown.

"Yeah."

"Not to speak ill of the dead, but why'd you want to borrow money off that shark in sheep's clothing?" Harry said.

"If Sean hadn't been unfairly dismissed from the Stone's Throw, he wouldn't be experiencing financial difficulties now," Mum said.

She always leaped to his defense. Some of us suspected his former employer had been rather more tolerant of my brother's faults than was warranted.

While Mum went on about *how hard he'd worked tending the bar* and Harry argued that *a stint in the armed forces would give him some spine*, I pinned my brother with my patented big sister glare. "How much?"

He spoke so softly that I had to strain to hear. "Ten grand."

"Ten *thousand* dollars?" I couldn't stop my voice from ratcheting up half an octave, which proved an effective means of silencing Harry and Mum.

No wonder Sean had wanted my advice; he was in way over his head.

My parents and Harry gaped at Sean in mute horror.

He sheepishly looked back. "I was working off the debt. It's not that big of a deal."

My mind backflipped to the bloody scene this morning and the chilly scrutiny I'd felt through the black lenses of Detective Mana's shades.

An employee with the means, opportunity, and in debt to the murdered man? It'd look like a big deal to him.

AFTER THAT, things went downhill fast.

Sean stormed out with Mum wailing after him like some maternal banshee, and Dad followed with an apologetic shrug. I didn't have the energy to mediate, as was my usual role within our family. Instead, I curled up in the vacated La-Z-Boy and let Harry make me a decent cup of tea. As early as non-pathetically possible, I excused myself and went to bed.

Sometime during the night, I woke to one cat nestled between my lax legs, the other on my chest, her purrs vibrating through my body. I scritched Pearl between her ears, and she gave a gigantic yawn before resuming her purring.

As one's brain is wont to do in the wee hours, my mind gnawed over the previous day's events and my brother's indebtedness to the victim of a violent crime. There was no way the police wouldn't find out about it and consider Sean a prime suspect. Especially with his checkered past...

Swearing softly under my breath, I carefully eased Pearl off my chest. I crept to the window and twitched back the drapes so I could see the street below. Nothing moved in the inky darkness, and the only sound was the soft sough of waves rolling ashore in the distance.

My stomach churned, and my thoughts were moths to a flame, returning over and over to Lucas Kerr and the bloodied knife. Surely, Sean couldn't be responsible. I had no idea why he owed his boss so much—he'd refused to answer Mum's hysterical questions. But I believed one thing wholeheartedly: The only circumstances in which my brother could kill would be in self-defense or to defend someone else.

I'd seen no evidence of a struggle in that back room; if anything, it indicated a level of premeditation. Someone, or *someones*, had shared a drink with Lucas last night. If that person was the same one who'd written the note and used him as a human corkboard, they'd taken the wine bottle and only one of the cups with them. By accident, I assumed. Any cold-blooded killer worth his or her salt wouldn't have left evidence behind.

Then there was the ransacked storeroom and the little bag of pills hidden inside a cheap cat ornament. Pills that I guessed would sell for a small fortune on the streets. Not exactly overwhelming evidence in favor of Sean's innocence.

I tried to convince myself that the police had this all under control. But thanks to my granddad, I knew that police were as human as the rest of us. And if they decided Sean was a person of interest, I couldn't allow my brother to be hauled through a system where suspects were often considered guilty until proven innocent.

However, what could I do? A former high school counselor who'd dealt with kids from all walks of life, with their family issues, peer issues, and self-esteem issues, I wasn't Sherlock in a skirt. I didn't have Miss Fisher's wiles or Poirot's steel-trap-like mind.

But...

I did know how to listen, not just to what someone was saying, but also to *how* they said it and what they didn't say. For whatever reason, people seemed to find me a convenient sounding board. I could use what skills I did have to poke around a bit, maybe see if I could unearth a few more suspects Detective Mana could sink his teeth into.

I tugged the drapes closed and crawled back into bed, the cats once again settling on me. It would be a while before I succumbed to the weariness making my eyelids droop, but I calmed myself by stroking Pearl's sleek fur in the meantime.

What harm could come of asking my neighbors a few innocent questions?

FIVE

The logical person to practice my interrogation skills on was the man I'd seen arguing with Lucas Kerr two days ago. After breakfast, I told Harry I needed to duck out to pick up a few groceries. Since Unraveled didn't open for another hour, I figured I had plenty of time to do some snooping.

I figured wrong.

What I hadn't factored in was every local in town descending on Hanburys to exchange gossip. The place was packed, with even Ed Hanbury working a checkout to cope with the rush. Bet he was rubbing his hands together over this influx of sales. I, however, had no intention of making it easy for the busybodies to extract gory details from the person who'd stumbled over a corpse yesterday morning. Turned out my fifteen minutes of fame wasn't as glamorous as I'd once envisaged.

Plan B, then.

Instead of going into the store, I walked around to the delivery entrance and the corner office next to it, where Ed's wife, Donna, worked. Spotting me, she waved me inside. I'd always liked Donna but often wondered how she'd managed to stay married for so long. Especially since they worked together all day, and he was, well, Ed.

"Hello, love. How're you doing?" Donna greeted me at her door and ushered me into the staff break room next to her office. "I'll put the kettle on, shall I?"

"Oh, you're probably too busy to stop with so many people shopping today."

"Rubbish. Ed won't deny me a coffee break; besides, he's in his element out there in the chaos. The man's a worse gossip than my old Aunt Cecilia—and that's saying something. Coffee or tea?"

I eyed the huge tin of coffee on the break room's counter. "Coffee for me, please. I'd mainline the stuff in the morning if I could."

Donna grinned. "I knew there was a reason I liked you. I'm a coffee addict too."

While she prepared our drinks, I made small talk, asking about their daughter and first grandchild. Another skill of mine was names and faces. Helpful when you work in a school of six hundred students and want to remember their names to help gain their trust.

Donna passed over a steaming mug and sat opposite me at the staff dining table. "Now, seriously. Did you sleep okay last night?" she asked.

"Not really. Knowing there's a murderer somewhere in town meant I kept hearing noises and thought they might be skulking outside." Not exactly why I couldn't switch off my brain, but close enough. "What about you?"

"I've worn earplugs for the past twenty-five years, so I didn't hear a thing." Donna nodded sagely. "I have to because if it's not Ed snoring, he's coming to bed late and crashing around the room. I sleep like the dead with them in." She clapped a hand over her mouth. "Oops. Didn't think."

I gave her a smile to reassure her I wasn't offended.

Her nose crinkled. "Ed's a night owl; I'm a morning person. He stays up late, while I struggle to stay awake past ten. But I'm up by five thirty most mornings."

"Yes, I'm a morning person too, although I sometimes can't resist the siren call of one more chapter when I'm reading at night." I sipped my coffee. "Is Ed a late-night reader?"

"Ed? Read a book?" She gave a soft snort. "Not hardly. He watches sport until late then takes Winnie out for a walk to do her business."

"Likes his routine, huh?"

"That he does. Gets a little cranky if the weather doesn't cooperate, and he can't go for his nightly stroll."

My mind leapfrogged back to Thursday evening and the flurry of umbrellas popping out of purses after the Crafting for Calmness class finished. "He must've been disappointed with the weather two nights ago."

"It was our twenty-fifth wedding anniversary on Thursday." She chuckled, a tinge of color rising in her cheeks. "I don't think he was too disappointed with the way the evening turned out."

"Oh, congratulations. Twenty-five years is amazing."

Hmm. And how had the evening turned out once Donna popped in her earplugs? Had Ed braved the intermittent showers to pay his arch business rival a visit? Had he spied a woman drinking wine with him through the store's back window, waited until she'd left, then attacked Lucas from behind?

"Did you do anything special to celebrate?" I asked.

"We went to The Royal Garden Thai that's just opened

in Napier. Have you heard of it? It's apparently very hard to get a table—oh! Ed." Donna clapped a hand to her heart. "You gave me such a fright."

My gaze shot sideways. Ed lurked in the doorway, his confused frown rapidly turning into a scowl.

Donna wagged a chiding finger. "Wipe that look off your face. I'm just taking my coffee break a bit early and having a nice chat with Tessa."

"Is that so?" His hawkish stare shifted to me. "Sounded like she was trying to find out if I had an alibi for the night of Lucas Kerr's murder."

"Don't be silly, love," Donna said.

"Don't be naïve, *love*," Ed replied. "Ms. Wakefield saw me arguing with him the other day, and she's wondering if that argument led to me offing him. It's no secret I disliked the man."

I didn't know Ed well, but you don't get to be vice-chairman of DOPE through sheer popularity. He was smart enough to see through my ruse, and I felt a little ashamed for subtly pumping Donna for information. However, not ashamed enough to not make the most of this opportunity, as I most likely wouldn't get another.

With men like Ed, who was a whisker away from being a schoolyard bully, if you could get them to boast and bluster a bit...

"Have the police interviewed you?" I asked. Bluntly.

Ed's chest visibly swelled as he folded his arms. "I've given them a statement, yes."

Wrinkling my nose in what I hoped came across as bored disdain, I picked up my mug. No need to look in his direction to know he was watching and waiting for a desperately interested reaction. He didn't get one. Instead, I blew on my coffee and took a sip.

He harrumphed after a few beats of strained silence. "I spoke to Detective Mana, who's in charge of this case. He's a straight-up bloke and doesn't beat around the bush."

"Oh?" I lifted one *maybe I'm interested in what you have to say* eyebrow. "Only an underling took my statement."

Ed couldn't keep the smirk from his mouth. "I immediately realized some might entertain the idea that I could be a suspect, so I nipped that in the bud by volunteering my alibi."

Another awkward pause while he waited for me to inquire what that alibi might be. Ask any teenager what they'd done when they snuck out of their room the night before, and I can pretty much guarantee you'll get a reply along the lines of 'nothing.'

I took another sip of coffee—which tasted surprisingly good for instant.

"Not that it's any of your business..." Ed began.

A-ha. Bingo!

"But we didn't arrive home from dinner until late, and after I took Winnie for a walk, I joined my wife in bed."

He jutted out his jaw as if daring me to make a risqué joke. But I had no interest in quizzing him about his anniversary shenanigans; I didn't want those unwelcome images seared into my brain. So I kept my mouth zipped. What time did Ed consider late? And how long was he out walking Winnie, an elderly and placid Labrador who'd happily snooze tied to a fencepost while her owner snuck into the old butcher shop?

As if reading my mind, Ed continued, "As I told Detective Mana, I was home by ten forty-five at the latest."

I slid Donna a side-eye and noticed a faint fan of wrinkles appear then disappear on her forehead. "Yes, it must've been around then. I dozed off, waiting for Ed and Winnie to get back." She addressed this statement in my direction. "But he woke me when he got home." Donna gave me a reassuring smile. "I guess because you had the unfortunate luck of finding poor Mr. Kerr, you're invested in finding out who would commit such a hideous crime?"

"Something like that." I wasn't prepared to admit my fears about my brother. "He was friendly toward me the few times I interacted with him."

Ed let out a derision-filled snort. "He was far too friendly with the town's ladies if you ask me. And he wasn't too fussy about whether that lady had a ring on her finger or not."

Huh. That put an interesting spin on the lipstick-smeared cup. "Lucas flirted with married women?" I asked.

"He didn't flirt with me," Donna said before Ed could answer.

Her husband didn't seem to pick up on the wistfully insulted note in her voice.

Ed nodded solemnly. "I was having a drink with Brian Werth and a few others at the Stone's Throw about a week ago."

"Brian Werth?"

"The dentist," Donna said helpfully. "He and his wife, Jennifer, moved into town about three years ago. They go to Saint Barnabas with us; they're a lovely couple—"

"Yes, yes. As I was saying," Ed continued, "Lucas walked in, and Brian gave him a filthy look. Nothing was said, at least not at the time. But I was the first to leave that evening, and Brian stayed on." He angled his head to look at me. "Talk to Oliver Novak. He was tending bar that night. If anything happened after I left, he'd know about it."

He gave a pointed glance at his wristwatch and sent a

dismissive look my way before returning his attention to his wife. "Break's over, dearest. I need you to take over for Sharon out front for a bit."

I thanked Donna for the coffee, reassured her I was fine, and remembering I still needed to pick up a few groceries, followed her into the store. She accompanied me as I snatched up a loaf of bread and some milk, providing a buffer from the curious stares that tracked me around the store. As I left his wife at the checkout, Ed's gaze burned into me. The prickle of it raised goosebumps down my spine.

While it seemed unlikely he'd commit homicide and then return home to his wife as if nothing had happened, I still couldn't scratch him off my mental list of suspects.

Turning my back on him made me irrationally nervous.

WHEN I GOT BACK, Harry was preparing to open the store. Earlier, he'd told me that I needed to take a couple of days off since I'd had a 'nasty fright,' and I hadn't argued. Reengaging with the store and the customers who stopped by to exchange gossip and, hopefully, buy yarn would do my granddad a world of good.

I put away the few grocery items I'd picked up, made him a cup of strong black tea, the way he liked it, and took it downstairs. Harry sat behind the service counter, wearing today's choice of beanie—black-and-white striped for the local rugby team. When I appeared with his tea, he shook out the newspaper he'd been reading and folded it.

"Wonderful." He gazed expectantly at the bulge in my shirt pocket.

With a grin, I pulled out two gingernut biscuits. "I didn't forget, but don't break your teeth."

Harry grinned back at me, proudly exposing his aged but well-maintained teeth. "You always were my favorite girl."

As if worried I might change my mind, he snatched the biscuits from my hand and dropped them into his own shirt pocket. "Speaking of favorite girls, I called a mate of mine from the Napier station. She couldn't tell me much about Lucas, only that he probably died somewhere between eleven and midnight. There was alcohol in his system, but they're waiting for the coroner's full report, including toxicology."

I swallowed hard. "Did your friend say how he died?"

Harry dipped his head to peer at me over the top of his reading glasses. "Multiple skull fractures, apparently."

"Do they know what was used?"

"She couldn't say officially, but her guess is a heavy glass object because there were a couple of tiny fragments in the wounds. You said you smelled wine in one of those cups you found?"

I nodded.

"There you go, then. Death by wine bottle. She also said the chef's knife ended up in him postmortem."

"He was already dead when someone stabbed him?"

"That's what it looks like."

"And the pills?" Over dinner last night, I'd told Harry about Pearl's discovery.

"Party pills. She mentioned there were other illegal substances found, but she wouldn't go into detail." He waved his hand. "Enough of this morbid talk. What are your plans today?"

If I told Harry what I intended to do—what I'd already

done by talking to Donna and Ed—I'd likely get a stern lecture on letting the professionals do their jobs. So I fudged the truth a little. "Thought I'll treat myself to lunch and maybe some shopping to support the local economy."

"About time you did something nice for yourself instead of running around looking after everyone else—me included."

I bent and kissed his grizzled cheek. "Someone has to keep you in line, old man."

"Who're you calling old?" He chuckled and waved me off. "Go on, then. I don't want to see hide nor hair of you until this afternoon."

I left via the back door, tiptoeing past Kit and Pearl, who were stretched out sunning themselves on the warm concrete path. The last thing I wanted was two cats trailing after me and getting into mischief.

The Stone's Throw sat on the corner of Crab—the cross street Unraveled was on—and the other main thoroughfare to the waterfront: Beach Street. Across from the pub, which was popular with locals but a little *too local* for most tourists, stood Saint Barnabas Church. Colloquially, it was referred to as Saint Barney's, a nickname that wouldn't go away, no matter how hard each resident vicar tried. The current vicar, Peter Salmon, kept his beady eye on the comings and goings from 'that sinful place across the way.'

I wasn't a fan of rough-around-the-edges pubs, so it'd been a long time since I'd set foot inside the Stone's Throw. Harry, not so much. He and Nana Dee-Dee used to be Friday night regulars, staying loyal to the place even when the new owner, Oliver Novak, took over last autumn. In fact, I'm sure it was Harry who'd got Sean a job there, and he'd taken it personally when it hadn't worked out. But unlike Mum, he blamed Sean, not Oliver, who he considered a 'decent enough bloke.'

Although the Stone's Throw didn't open until mid-afternoon, I hoped this Oliver guy might be on the premises anyway. The battered SUV parked in the service lane behind the pub in a 'Staff Only' parking spot seemed a good sign. I decided to chance knocking on the service door instead of being ignored as a pesky early customer at the front.

As I approached the solid door, currently propped open with a brick, loud eighties rock music pumped from within. Unless I produced a handy sledgehammer, nobody would hear me politely knocking.

I peered into the dim interior: a hallway lined with stacked boxes of booze. I had a moment's concern that Sean's comment about his former boss keeping a baseball bat behind the bar in case of trouble wasn't a joke. Respect for the bat made me rap on the door before I stepped inside. No response.

"Hello?" My voice was swallowed up by a guitar solo.

I followed the music through another propped-open door and into the pub itself, where I stuttered to a halt, my jaw almost hitting the scuffed-up hardwood floor. The standing tables and stools had been pushed to one side for mopping to take place, and the mopper—who'd taken center stage with his, well...mop—was performing an air guitar solo. Now, while I appreciate a good air guitar as much as the next fan of mullet-headed eighties rockers, it was the man himself that caused my salivary glands to perk up.

Tall, with the physique of an athlete that trained hard but not blown up to the ridiculous proportions of a bodybuilder, he filled his snug T-shirt and faded blue jeans to perfection. No wonder Nana Dee-Dee had always returned from the Stone's Throw in a good mood if this guy was one of the staff. "I may be old," she'd say when I caught her grinning at the Bachelorette's suitors, "but I've still got my eyesight and a pulse."

This unexpected memory of my nana reminded me of why I was here. For my family.

I cupped my hands around my mouth and hollered, "Excuse me."

At the exact same instant as the song ended.

The man dropped his mop and spun around so fast I let out a noise somewhere between a goat scream and a giant hiccup. I stumbled back a step, tripped on my flip-flop, and was only saved the humiliation of falling by flinging out a hand to grab the bar edge. In doing so, I knocked over an open box of potato chips. Packets of salt 'n' vinegar—my number one favorite flavor—cascaded to the floor.

Graceful spatial awareness—not one of my strong suits.

Once I'd regained my balance, I held up *please don't kill me* palms. "Sorry. I did knock, but..."

That statement earned me a look clearly questioning the sanity of knocking when the music's volume was loud enough to vibrate the pub's walls. Hyperbole, I know, but it sure felt that way. As the next track's guitar intro blasted out, he dug in his jeans pocket, pulled out his phone, and tapped the screen. The room went silent.

"We open at eleven."

He didn't seem at all perturbed by being caught boogying with a mop, but me being me, I blushed for him. "I know. Again, *sorry*. I just wanted a quick word with your boss; if he's around?"

"My boss?" He strode toward me and into a patch of sunlight streaming through a skylight above the bar.

Up close and facing forward, he was even yummier

than in the distance and from behind. Sandy blond hair, due for a trim, a playboy's jaw, and a glimpse of ink peeking out from under the neckline of his T-shirt. Yummy, and more than a little impatient because, you know, he had his screaming groupies to get back to.

"Yeah, Oliver Novak. Is he around?" Admittedly, a dumb question because what boss did scut work when they had an underling to do it instead?

The man's eyes narrowed as he studied my face. "Are you one of Sean's sisters?"

Ah. So this must be Sean's *replacement*.

Though he knew my brother? Probably by reputation, so, ugh. Also, ugh that I resembled my brother enough that this guy could pick up on inherited genetic traits. Darn you, curly hair, blue eyes, and a knack for being in the wrong place at the wrong time.

But there was no point in denying our relationship.

"Yes, I am. Tessa Wakefield." I shot out a hand for him to shake.

He moved his foot in a nifty soccer move, caught the bag of chips he'd flicked up, and pushed them into my palm. "Oliver Novak. You wanna restack these?" His greeny-blue eyes were the exact shade of a new yarn called Spellbound that I'd ordered last week. And I was, for a moment, spellbound when his gaze locked with mine.

This was Oliver? Not the late-forty-something man with curly gray hair, blue shirt, and a bowtie that I'd imagined on the walk here? Okay, I admit, I was picturing Moe from *The Simpsons*—so sue me.

I must have been gawping like a goldfish because laugh lines suddenly radiated from those pretty eyes. "Please?" he added.

I clicked my back teeth together and dropped my gaze

to the scattered packets. Just then, my stomach vocalized its displeasure at missing out on morning tea and gingernuts.

Oliver laughed, but it was a kind laugh, not a mocking one. "Chuck them back in the box, and I'll split one with you while you tell me what I can help you with."

"Deal." As I crouched to scoop up the packets, Oliver headed behind the bar.

Once I'd set the box to rights—minus one packet because I never look a gift horse in the mouth when it comes to snacks—I leaned against the end of the bar.

"Beer?" He turned with two bottles in his hand.

I was about to shake my head but remembered alcohol's loosening effect on the tongue. "Thanks."

He cracked open both bottles and passed me one, which I promptly latched onto like a greedy orphan lamb. With any luck, the cool liquid would quench my sizzling cheeks.

I set the bottle down after a long draw and opened my mouth, my line of questioning all planned out on the walk to the pub. Instead, what emerged was, "Do you think my brother is capable of murder?"

SIX

"I think everyone's capable of killing another human being in certain circumstances," Oliver said with a nonchalance that suggested he often fielded such questions from women who gatecrashed his pub in the middle of the day.

Since I hadn't intended to blurt out my deepest fear to a stranger, I muttered, "Okay."

He sent me a probing look from behind the bar and reached over it to pluck the bag of chips from my hand. Once opened, he offered me first pick.

I selected the largest unbroken one, its salty-vinegary smell making my taste buds sit up and beg. About to bite into it, I had an epiphany—there was no way to eat a potato chip without sounding like a wood chipper chewing through a dead tree. With a mental shrug, I bit into the tasty morsel anyway. I'd more important things to worry about than crunching chips in front of a man so far out of my league it'd take a zombie apocalypse where I was the sole undead woman in town for him to consider me dateable.

Oliver, who clearly had no qualms about noisy snacking,

crunched down on a chip. His eyes smiled at me as we munched in surprisingly companionable silence. After we'd decimated the pack—he proved he was a good bloke when he let me have the last one—he pressed a paper napkin into my hand.

"Figured we'd think better on a full stomach." He cocked his head. "Do *you* believe Sean's capable of murder?" he asked gently.

"No. But as his sister, I'm genetically wired to believe that." I met his curious gaze. "You've no emotional connection to him; in fact, I'm guessing you two didn't get on, since you fired him."

Oliver crumpled the empty chip packet and tossed it into a nearby trashcan. When he turned back to face me, he leaned forward and rested his folded arms on the polished wooden bar. "I didn't let Sean go because we didn't get on," he said. "Is that what he told you?"

"He doesn't say much at all," I admitted. "At first, he muttered about differences of opinion, how it was your way or the highway type of thing, and said he would've quit if you hadn't fired him first. Now he clams up on the subject whenever it's raised."

Oliver nodded, as if that was the response he'd expected.

"Why did you let him go?" I asked.

"It's not my place to give away his secrets."

I swallowed hard. "Sean has secrets?"

"Everyone has secrets, Tessa."

The way he said my name sent a delicious shiver down my spine.

"Can you at least tell me if Sean's secret could get him arrested for murder?"

He sighed and rubbed a finger along the cleft of his

chin, making a soft scritching sound against his heavy stubble. "Maybe."

"Something to do with the large amount of money he owes?" I pressed, even though I suspected a guy like Oliver wouldn't be pushed into doing or saying anything he didn't want to.

Oliver quirked an eyebrow. "Don't you think you should be asking your brother this?" He drained his beer and tucked the empty bottle out of sight behind the counter. Then he picked up a damp cloth and ran it over the already spotless bar surface.

Polite chitchat over, hint, hint.

Message received, loud and clear. However, I still needed to ask one more question before I left.

And no, it wasn't 'are you single?'

"Were you tending bar about a week ago when Ed Hanbury was drinking here?" I posed it as a question, as, for some reason, I trusted Oliver to tell me the truth, but not Ed.

"I tend bar most nights," he said. "But yeah, I remember Ed and his friends. They're not exactly frequent-flyers."

I slid a glance around the room, fitted out in quintessential Old New Zealand Pub style. Low ceiling with reclaimed wood rafters, giant TV mounted at one end for sports fans, and a battered pool table at the opposite end. There were few decorative touches because people came here to drink and socialize, not to order dirty martinis and evaluate artwork on the wall. "No offense, but this doesn't strike me as an Ed Hanbury kind of place."

Oliver smiled, and wow, did he have a bone-jellifying smile. "No offense taken. Your grandparents like it well enough." His smile slipped. "I was sorry to hear about Nana Dee-Dee. I miss Mrs. G-and-T as I used to call her."

"Thank you." A knot formed in my stomach. Mrs. G- and-T. She would've loved that nickname.

"You were asking about Ed?" he prompted a few beats of silence later.

"He told me there might've been some sort of confrontation between Lucas Kerr and another customer that evening."

"Ah. Lucas. The unfortunate dead guy." His smile returned. "I thought Sean had an older sister who's a high school guidance counselor, not a detective."

"I'm just naturally curious."

"That could get you into trouble."

"Why, Mr. Novak. Is that a threat?"

He chuckled. "It's Oliver or Ollie. And more a suggestion to tread lightly." His expression turned serious. "Someone killed Lucas, and unless they're a complete sociopath, they're scared the cops will find them. Scared people can lash out at an easy target. Cops aren't easy targets, but you are."

"I'll be careful. Now, back to Lucas and Brian Werth? Tell me exactly what happened."

A frustrated sigh as Oliver tossed the cleaning cloth aside and braced his spread-out arms on the bar. "The pub had started to empty near closing, and there were only a few bodies still warming their barstools. I left Mac behind the bar and went to check the bathrooms. I found Brian and Lucas outside the Men's. Brian's a big guy for a dentist, yeah?"

I nodded, having seen him in passing. It'd be like having the Incredible Hulk looming over you, his big mitt wrapped around the tiny buzzing device he intended to cram in your mouth. Fortunately, my genes had bequeathed me healthy teeth and gums, and I hadn't required the man's services. Yet.

"Brian had Lucas pinned to the wall by the throat. He got all up in his face and told him to stay away from his family."

"Jealous husband?" I wondered aloud.

"Couldn't say. Though he looked at Lucas like he'd happily extract all his teeth for free—with his fists."

"What was Lucas doing? Protesting his innocence?"

"He didn't say a word. Just stared up at Brian with his mouth frozen in a sneer." Oliver rolled his shoulders. "Brain noticed me and let Lucas go. He stormed back along the hallway, and I heard the pub door slam as he left. Lucas straightened his shirt and stared after him with that same condescending sneer. 'After a few drinks, some men just can't control themselves,' he said."

Oliver's mouth twisted. "'Or their woman,' I thought I heard him say as he pushed past me."

"Thought you heard?"

"It was late, and I'd covered an extra shift for one of my employees. I might've misheard."

Husband suspects local shopkeeper of slipping it to his wife and murders him—staging the scene to make it appear unrelated to marital jealousy. I toyed with the theory for a moment and declared it plausible. But not fully formed enough to wave under Detective Mana's nose and point him in a different direction.

"Interesting." I slid the three-quarters full beer bottle across the bar. "Thanks for the beer and chips."

"You're welcome." He straightened to his full height and folded his arms across his chest. Muscles bunched left, right, and center, distracting me for an embarrassing stretch of time. I shouldn't have had those five sips of beer.

"Why don't you bring Harry down for Happy Hour sometime?" he asked.

"Sure."

At that point, I would have agreed to almost anything to make a quick exit while I still retained some tiny shred of feminine mystique. Mystique being the ability to leave the pub without tripping over my feet or giggling like some teenage girl when the cutest boy in school gives her a nod of acknowledgment in the cafeteria.

I backed away from the bar, dithering over whether I should leave like a customer, via the front door, or go out the way I'd come in. The latter seemed overfamiliar. Customer, I decided and scurried to the front door. Which was secured with a series of Fort Knox–worthy locks, all conspiring to make me look as uncoordinated as I actually was while unlocking them. Finally, after much trial and error and a substantial amount of rattling, I wrenched the door open.

"Nice to meet you, Tessa," Oliver called out from behind me, laughter rippling through his deep voice.

I spun back to him with a flustered, "You too." And, inexplicably, a thumbs up.

Restraining my runaway hands from performing a double face-palm next, I hotfooted it out of the Stone's Throw and headed toward the beach. Where I intended to throw myself off the pier. But before that, and before I could change my mind, I found the Discovery Dental Surgery number online and left a request on their answering service for a Monday morning appointment.

The sacrifices you make for family.

My phone tinkled merrily as I went to drop it back into my pocket. The only actual calls I received now were marketers, Harry butt-dialing me because he'd sat on his phone (yet again), or my mother, who thought sending a text to her children was tantamount to parental neglect. Running through a mental list of excuses I could use to avoid listening to a Mum rant, I peered at the caller's name on the screen.

It was Sean. Who'd need to be held at gunpoint before using any form of communication other than text message or email.

I frowned at it for another couple of beats before tapping 'Accept.'

"Tess? I didn't know who else to call." My brother's voice bleated out of the speaker. "I'm at the police station in Napier." At his ragged inhalation, my stomach plummeted. "They want to ask me more questions about Lucas's murder."

WHEN YOUR BROTHER NEEDS YOU, even when that brother can be a right royal pain in the rear, you drop everything and go.

At least, that's what I do. What I've always done when my family needs me.

Mum gets her grandchild a plush toy birthday gift more suitable for a toddler than a twelve-year-old; I calm second oldest sister, Kelly, with assurances that a tween's not going to like anything her grandmother gets her. Eldest sister, Jill, gets huffy when Sean rags on her husband about his new luxury SUV; I remind her that Sean can go on boring fishing trips with his brother-in-law, so she doesn't have to.

I sprinted home, jumped in my car, and pointed it toward the city.

Napier Police Station—which from the outside looks more like a modern public library, minus the books and smiling librarians—made my heart stampede under my ribs. I walked inside, and if I'd had boots on, I'd have been shaking in them. After a brief conversation at the reception desk, I sat down to wait for an officer to brief me.

But I didn't get an officer; I got Detective Mana himself.

Or perhaps that should be himself with a capital H.

I'm sure I wasn't the only civilian in the station that gave him a second, and possibly third, glance as he strode across the foyer. He wore dress pants—not charcoal, these were more thundercloud gray. Was it casual Friday? Because in a button-down shirt with the sleeves rolled up to his elbows, he was minus a suit jacket.

However, the detective's attire, and admittedly, he knew how to work a good tailoring job, wasn't as distracting as I'd have liked. All the nerves clamoring in my stomach fizzed as I sprang to my feet. Lightheadedness turned his dark hair fuzzy around the edges but brought his eyes into crystal-clear focus. They were chips of dirty ice, a pale, penetrating gray that had me swaying under their intensity.

Strong fingers gripped my elbow. "Are you all right?"

Nope, not all right. I was positively all wrong.

I blinked a couple of times, clearing the fogginess in my brain. For the second time today, my stomach gave a loud, protesting growl.

Seriously, universe? This was how you rewarded me for not burying my ex in a shallow grave and putting up with my family's shenanigans? By turning my own bodily functions against me when in the company of good-looking, possibly single, men?

Still. There were more embarrassing involuntary bodily functions...

I forced a weak smile. But before I could reassure the detective with a hackneyed, 'I'm fine,' he gave me a speculative frown, those cool gray eyes taking X-ray images of my face to analyze.

"You haven't had lunch, Ms. Wakefield."

It hadn't been framed as a question, but I answered anyway. "No. I drove straight down from Cape Discovery. I don't snack and drive, Detective Mana."

"Pleased to hear it." He finally released my elbow, and I had to forcibly restrain myself from rubbing my fingers over the residual warmth on my skin. Cocking his head and looking eerily like a giant bird of prey spotting a small but tasty rodent, he said, "There's a café a couple of doors down from the station. You should eat." A dimple flickered in his cheek. "Before you get behind the wheel again."

He must have caught my glance shifting over his shoulder to the *Inaccessible to the Public* doors leading into the inner sanctum of cops. "Your brother's still being interviewed, Ms. Wakefield, but he won't be too much longer."

That was positive, wasn't it? He hadn't been arrested at least, but I was desperate to know what direction the investigation was taking. And that desperation gave me a boldness boost. "Have *you* had lunch, Detective Mana?"

His dark eyebrows twerked upward before settling back into what I was beginning to think of as his default expression—a slight 'V' of a frown.

"As it happens, no. It's been a hectic morning." The 'V' deepened. "And you don't have to keep calling me Detective Mana. It's Eric."

Eric.

I turned the name over in my mind. There was guitarist Eric Clapton, actor Eric Dane, and let's not forget the fictional vampire Eric Northman from *True Blood*. It was a serious, teeny bit intimidating name, and it suited him.

"You do look a bit hangry, Eric." Which, come to think

of it, might be an explanation for his default frown. Big guy like him would need a lot of fuel to keep running. "Want to join me?"

"For...lunch?"

A snarky comeback was on the tip of my tongue, but I swallowed it. I needed the detective...*Eric*...to like me. Okay, not *like me* like me, but not want to arrest me either. "Yes. You do eat, right?"

I hadn't managed to keep all the snark out of my voice, but his frown smoothed, and I got another dimple flash.

"Most days." He gestured toward the exit. "Guess I can spare a few minutes."

I slid a glance over at him on the way to the door. "If you can eat lunch in a few minutes, you might want to invest in some indigestion tablets."

With his longer legs, Eric still managed to reach the door before me; he pinned it open. "When you come from a family of six boys, you learn to eat fast or miss out."

"Oh." My gaze shot to his face, but at some point while crossing the station foyer, he'd slipped on his wraparound shades. That he'd volunteered this tiniest scrap of personal information left me momentarily flummoxed. Eric Mana didn't strike me as the type of guy to share anything but the cold, hard facts. "Five brothers? Wow. That must've been..."

As his eyebrows rose slowly above his shades, I realized I'd stalled in the middle of the doorway. Yeah. I should probably stop gawking at him if I planned to pump the man for information about my brother.

Giving a nervous *oopsie* chuckle, I scuttled out of the way. When I hesitated at the bottom of the entrance ramp, his deep voice came from above. "Left," he commanded.

Like a good little sheep, I turned left and headed along

the sidewalk. Eric fell into step beside me but said nothing; he just gave a nonverbal grunt when we reached the café.

Thanks to the lunchtime rush being over, the place was almost empty. We ordered from the counter, and since I was served first, I chose a booth near the back. After folding himself into the seat opposite, Eric set his phone, shades, and wallet on the table. He laced his fingers together, his cool gray gaze never leaving my face.

"My brother didn't kill Lucas Kerr."

If he really did only have a few minutes before returning to the on-the-record detective sergeant of the New Zealand Police doing his job, I didn't have time to make polite chitchat. To his credit, my bluntness didn't appear to disconcert him.

"Your reasoning behind this statement?" he said mildly. But his swift return to formality was a stark reminder that Eric Mana was a cop first, human being second.

I needed to keep my guard locked in the 'up' position.

"Aside from Sean being as squeamish as a kid watching their first horror movie, he had no motive."

Did he know about Sean's indebtedness to Lucas?

"Your brother had borrowed a substantial amount of money off his employer."

Yep. He did. I didn't want to admit that I also knew.

Under the table, I squeezed my hands into tight fists. "How much are we talking about? A couple of grand?"

"Ten thousand dollars."

I theatrically crinkled my nose. "Hardly worth killing someone over."

"That's just the tip of the iceberg." He leaned back in his seat as the server set down an espresso for Eric and a pot of peppermint tea for me.

"What do you mean 'tip of the iceberg'?" I demanded once the server walked away.

Eric shook a sachet of sugar to loosen it, tore it open, stared at it as if it'd magically appeared in his hands, then folded over the torn edge and placed it neatly on the edge of his saucer. Once again, his chilly gaze found mine. "Your brother has a serious gambling problem. Lucas isn't the only person Sean owes money to."

His statement made no sense. "Sean doesn't gamble—I mean, no more than any of us. He buys a lottery ticket religiously, and his idea of a good birthday or Christmas gift is a couple of scratchies in a greeting card..."

The chill in his eyes melted to what I could only describe as pity. The kind of pity one feels for someone making an idiot of themselves because they're in complete denial of the obvious.

The server returned with the rest of our order: a toasted ham and cheese sandwich for me and a roast vegetable and chicken salad for Eric. She smiled at him, but seeming not to notice, he dismissed her with a polite but curt, "Thank you."

"It's more than that, Ms. Wakefield,' he said as the woman returned to her spot behind the counter, shooting him the occasional dejected glance. "He started with the pokies, moved on to online gambling, then became an informal bookie, which put him in the crosshairs of some vicious people."

"Tessa," I said, taking from those sentences the only thing I could cope with. "Since you've lobbed a grenade into our family, you might as well do it on a first-name basis."

If I'd waited for him to apologize, my toasted sandwich would've gone cold. Eric sipped his coffee, calmly watching me try to piece together this new information. I just couldn't seem to get from point A: *Sean owed more than ten thousand dollars* to B: *Lucas Kerr dead*. Not with a police detective studying my face.

I sucked in a deep breath and poured myself a cup of peppermint tea. "Sean told you all this?"

"He did," Eric said, caution slowing his response. "And having a gambling addiction isn't, in and of itself, a crime. But added to other evidence we discovered at the crime scene, it does give him a motive."

Steam rose from my cup as I lifted it to my lips, and I narrowed my eyes in response.

Actually, I was giving the detective my best stabby glare. Not that he noticed. "Like the drugs in Lucas's storeroom. I'm guessing the pills my cat found weren't the only ones in there."

"They weren't, no."

"Then isn't it possible"—I lowered my cup a fraction—"that someone who isn't my brother killed him to get hold of those drugs? A gang or a rival dealer? That could explain the 'get out of town' note." I warmed to my alternative theory. "Ooh. Or the drugs and the note might have been to throw you guys off the trail of whoever left the lipstick-smeared cup at the scene."

"Noticed that, did you?" Eric said dryly.

"I also heard Lucas noticed a lot of women in town. That he might've been a little *too friendly* toward some of them. Women who had men in their lives that might strongly object to a harmless flirtation. Or more than a harmless flirtation." I gave him the raised-brow knowing look. "Isn't it *possible* there are others in Discovery Cove who wanted Mr. Kerr dead more than my brother?"

Like the leprechaun pin's owner.

I didn't dwell on that because I was most likely breaking

a multitude of laws by not handing it in to the authorities. But in my defense, odds were the pin had nothing to do with murder and everything to do with party supplies the pop-up store stocked.

Eric's mouth pinched shut. "It's possible," he said after a moment. "And we've just begun our investigation." He stiffened, setting his cup back down on the saucer with a clink. "I can't discuss any more of this case with you. We should eat and get back to the station."

"Okey-dokey." I picked up my sandwich without further comment.

Maybe I'd planted the seed that Sean Wakefield wasn't the only potential suspect in town. I just hoped I'd done a good enough job of helping it grow some roots.

SEVEN

The drive back to Discovery with my brother took, oh, about two thousand hours. At least, that's what it felt like trapped in my car with him. From the moment we'd walked out of the police station, he'd reverted to his fourteen-year-old self. With an everything-and-everyone-sucks attitude, he communicated in monosyllabic words and a range of disdainful grunts.

I gave up on conversation after twenty minutes of trying to elicit a rational response. But unless he snapped out of this sulky silence, we stood little chance of figuring out what had really happened to Lucas Kerr. As a school counselor, I'd peeled apart fourteen-year-old boys like onions during a couple of sessions in my office. However, with the possibility of my brother being arrested on a murder charge, time and coddling were luxuries I lacked.

Sean sat hunched in the passenger seat, his arms folded and his shoulders near his ears as he faked a nap.

"I had an interesting lunch with Detective Mana." I overtook a farmer's ute. Two smiling sheepdogs sat on the flatbed, their tongues lolling in the slipstream.

His eyes flew open as he bolted upright. "You had lunch with who?"

"Detective Mana." We both knew he'd heard the first time. "But he said I should call him Eric."

Sean's jaw sagged.

Good, I had his undivided attention.

"*Eric* is aware of your debt and described you as having a gambling problem. Is that a fair assessment?"

I got an affirmative grunt as a reply.

Oliver's voice popped up in my brain: *It's not my place to give away his secrets.*

"Is gambling the reason you lost your job at the Stone's Throw?"

His jaw bunched like he was biting down on a leather strap. "Yeah."

"Do Mum and Dad know?"

A negative grunt. He grimaced, blowing out a *may as well get it over with* sigh. "I'd maxed out my credit card playing online poker, so I ramped up taking under-the-table bets at the pub. Ollie gave me a warning and a second chance, but when he had to step in one night to stop a sore-loser client from breaking my fingers..." My brother shrugged. "He told me to get out and get my act together. I've been trying to do that."

"And Lucas just happened to offer you a job days after you left the pub?"

Sean frowned. "He was there the night the guy nearly broke my hand. When I saw the help wanted sign in the old butcher shop window and applied, he must've recognized me and felt sorry for me." His frown deepened. "Now I think about it, Lucas didn't ask too many questions before he told me I was hired."

How could Sean not realize how suspicious that

sounded?" "And out of the goodness of his heart, he loans a huge amount of money to a complete stranger only a few weeks later?"

"It wasn't huge to Lucas, and we weren't strangers by then."

Guess ten thousand wasn't a lot if most of your income came from illegal activities.

"What were you? *Friends*?"

"Nah. I wouldn't say we were friends. More like mates. Y'know. Wanna go for a beer at the end of the day, *mate*? Or, *mate*, wanna give me a heads-up if one of those crazy chicks comes in looking for me again?"

"Or, *mate*, can I borrow ten grand to stop some other guy from breaking my fingers *and* my legs?"

"Do you always have to be so judgy?" Sean grumbled. "Can't a mate let another mate help him out without being given the fifth degree?"

"Third degree."

"Whatever degree. He was just being a mate."

Not if that mate happened to be murdered and thousands of dollars' worth of illegal drugs found on the premises. Instead of defending my judginess, I opted for an out-of-the-blue question. "Did the store stock any Saint Patrick's Day decorations?"

A grunt, followed by, "It's not the time to be worrying about how you'll decorate Unraveled for Saint Paddy's Day."

A complete sentence—progress. "Maybe. But do you have those clover party favors, sparkly green hats... leprechaun pins?"

"What? It's only January, so no. Anyway, unless Lucas had decided to stay, he would've shut up shop and moved on to another town by the beginning of March."

"Where he'd start selling drugs to another community?"

A loaded silence from my brother. "I didn't know he was dealing, Tess."

"Okay." But to be honest, I wasn't entirely sure I believed him.

Slowing for a buildup of traffic, I glanced over at Sean. He scrubbed a hand tiredly over his face in an unguarded moment. Regardless of what he'd done in the past or whether he wasn't telling the truth about Lucas's side business, I knew down to my marrow that my brother hadn't killed his boss. Not that Detective Mana and his police brethren would rely on familial intuition. And I had no idea if they were seriously looking at anyone other than Sean.

I replayed my earlier conversation with Oliver Novak about Brian Werth's jealous rage—and recalled something Sean had said earlier. "Who was the crazy chick Lucas wanted a heads-up about?"

"There was more than one. When I saw him at the Stone's Throw that first time, he was at a corner table, perfecting his lone-wolf act. Women got sucked in by it like dust bunnies into a vacuum. Lucas never had trouble finding female company."

Nice. The victim had been a sleazy player…but that also widened the suspect pool. "Anyone in particular you can think of?"

"Why are you suddenly interested in my boss's love life? I mean, my *former* boss's love life."

As I took the Cape Discovery turnoff, I mentally counted to ten, so I wouldn't smack my little brother upside the head. "I am trying…" I said with as much patience as I could muster, "to figure out who in town has more motive than you to kill Lucas."

"Oh. Gotcha. You don't trust the cops to do that?"

"Do you?"

Sean bumped back against the headrest a couple of times and then slumped down in his seat. "Yeah, nah."

The blue line of the ocean in the distance broadened as my car hugged the winding curves down toward the beach. Sunlight sparkled off the water's flat surface, making it appear crystal clear. And not for the first time, I realized my hometown, which I'd always seen as like the ocean itself, was actually murky, churning with hidden dangers beneath.

"There was this one woman Lucas did his best to avoid. He called her Velcro," Sean said. "I don't know her name."

"What did she look like?"

"A normal middle-aged woman, I dunno."

Anyone over the age of forty would be 'middle-aged' by Sean's definition. So *not* helpful. "Anything else you remember? What she wore? Hair and eye color? Attractive?"

"Normal middle-aged woman clothes. No idea—maybe brown to both? And, again, I dunno."

Given that it was Sean, I'd believe he was pretty clueless about female apparel. Ditto hair and eye color. But a good-looking woman... "You didn't notice if she was attractive? *Really?*"

A deadpan stare. "Cougars aren't my thing."

Ignoring his piggish response, I focused on the hint of a clue to the woman's identity. "She was older than Lucas?"

"Like I said, a cougar. Yeah, I think Lucas was around your age. She was definitely old—I mean, *older*."

Not much to go on, but it was a start.

While driving into Cape Discovery, I mentally compiled a list of women I knew over the age of forty. A deep suspect pool; so, again, *not* helpful. I parked outside the house where my brother rented a small downstairs apartment and left the engine running.

Sean climbed out of the car, slammed the door, and then leaned in through the open passenger window. "Someone else that showed up at the store a few times was the dentist's son." He drummed his fingers on the sill. "He's in high school but not one of those foul-mouthed skateboarding brats that travel in packs. Dylan, I think his name is. Maybe you should try to find out why a quiet, studious kid like him was hanging around Lucas. Anyway"—straightening, he rapped his knuckles on the roof of my car—"thanks for the ride."

After a half dozen steps toward his house, Sean paused, turned back. "Thanks for more than the ride, Tess. Just... thank you."

I waved him off with a smile, even though I was absurdly touched by this small crumb of appreciation.

When I arrived home, I was greeted by matching yowls of demand for chin scratches and treats—not necessarily in that order. Pearl and Kit accompanied me up the stairs, perilously twining around my ankles. I walked into the living room, kissed Harry's head—still covered in his black-and-white beanie, which had slipped down over his eyes as he snoozed in front of the TV—and curled up in Nana Dee-Dee's chair.

By the time I'd pulled needles and yarn from the knitting basket beside the chair, Kit had launched himself onto my lap while Pearl perched on the back above my head. From there, she stared disdainfully at the partially knitted fingerless glove dangling from one needle. As I knitted and purled, I pondered how to talk to the dentist's son without arousing suspicion. School was out for at least another two weeks, and I had no idea where Dylan—or any teenage boy for that matter—spent their long summer days.

I nearly dropped a stitch.

Thanks to Donna Hanbury, I *did* know where Dylan and his parents would be tomorrow morning. And I planned to be there too.

However, this prodigal daughter might be welcomed with a stray bolt of lightning when she returned.

PETER SALMON, the current vicar of Saint Barnabas, didn't think much of me. Whenever our paths crossed, he'd smile and give me an acknowledging nod. But his expression was one a polite person assumed when entering a room someone had farted in moments before.

I wasn't sure whether it was because he didn't approve of my family's sporadic attendance at Saint Barney's, or if he still hadn't forgiven me for laughing when he'd announced two Christmas Eve services ago that he was starting an Aerobics for the Almighty class in the new year. It had been a knee-jerk reaction—and, hey, it was bad enough the vicar power walked his sixty-plus-years-old bod around town in way too much Lycra every morning.

This Sunday, I planned to be on my best behavior.

Slipping into the very back pew with only a minute to spare before the service began, I scanned the rows in front. Two rows ahead, I spotted the recently clipped hair of a young man with protruding sunburned ears and hunched shoulders. A woman with dark hair held back with an Alice band bookended him on one side, a mountain-shouldered man on the other. The dentist's bulk was unmistakable.

Jackpot.

I relaxed, as much as one can, into the wooden pew. Don't ask me what that morning's sermon was about. The vicar had a voice worthy of a world-renowned hypnotist, and five minutes in, I was ready to quit my potato chip addiction and cluck like a chicken. I zoned out between hymns, which Peter's organ-playing wife accompanied. Her performance style swung from all the enthusiasm of a Broadway production to a zombie death march. I wondered briefly if she provided the music for Aerobics for the Almighty.

Thankfully, the service eventually finished with a great flourishing huzzah from Mrs. Salmon and the pianist, who looked somewhat miffed at being drowned out by the organ. The vicar invited the congregation for morning tea and fellowship in the church hall. Not feeling particularly fellowshippy, I avoided any chitchat or curious gazes by ducking outside. I slunk around the side of the church to where I had a fine view of the hall's entrance.

Every churchgoer—even an infrequent one such as myself—knows if you want a shot at a slice of banana cake or a melting moment biscuit, you have to beat the rush of people with the same idea. First come, first served. Fellowship could wait until after tea and home baking.

Sure enough, a few parishioners had already hurried out of Saint Barney's back exit and were hotfooting it along the path—including Dylan Werth. With his lanky stride, he easily overtook a mauve-coated lady using a walker. But obviously raised with some manners, he pinned the hall door open and let her enter first.

If I knew teenagers, and I did...

Leaning back against the church's brick wall, I waited. Dylan reappeared less than a minute later, cradling a paper napkin in his hands as if it contained the crown jewels.

There was no way any teenager would voluntarily stay in a room with their parents and other 'old' people if there was an option of escape.

After a quick glance back at the church, he took off in the opposite direction, heading toward the old graveyard that sloped down to the boundary wall. I followed. By the time I'd stepped around a giant weeping angel monument, Dylan had settled on the stone wall to devour what appeared to be a large wedge of carrot cake. He had a smear of cream cheese frosting on his nose.

"That cake looks good."

He squinted up at me. "It is."

I went to sit a socially appropriate distance away from him on the wall, but there was no way my cute but impractical slim-fitting linen dress would permit the maneuver. I ended up in an awkward lean against one of the evenly spaced wall pillars. "Best part of church, huh?"

This asked as one of my pointy heels sank into a soft patch of earth. I yanked it out again and stood like a flamingo.

"Yup." Dylan continued to methodically work his way through the cake, his face conveying how embarrassing it would be to be seen talking to someone over the age of twenty.

Tough luck, kiddo.

I calculated I had maybe fifteen minutes max to pry any useful information out of the boy before one of his parents came looking.

"You're the dentist's son?"

Another squinty-eyed peek over the frosting. "Stepson." He hooked a finger over his shirt's stiff white collar, tugging it away from his bobbing Adam's apple. "He's my stepdad."

Something I hadn't known. "Oh." I dipped my chin at

the last few mouthfuls of cake. "Guess he wouldn't approve of all that sugar you've just consumed."

His freckled nose crinkled. "In our house, dessert is a four-letter word."

I grinned at him. "Your secret's safe with me."

While I contemplated how to switch topics from cake to corpse, Dylan licked frosting off his fingers then swiped his shirt cuff across his mouth. "Are you the lady who found the dead guy on Friday?"

"Uh-huh." Interesting that he'd referred to Lucas as 'the dead guy.' Like he hadn't known him. Another trick I'd learned was to not get up into teenagers' faces when you suspected they were lying.

"You knew Lucas a little?" Before he could lie, I added, "My brother worked at the store, and he saw you there a few times." I embellished with an *it's not important; just making conversation* shrug and stared across the road to where a man was getting ready to mow his front lawn.

Dylan cleared his throat. "Yeah. Um, Lucas is an okay guy...*was* an okay guy." I could feel the boy's gaze on the side of my face, searching for a reaction or some sort of clue as to how I expected *him* to react.

Unlike young Dylan, I had a satisfactory poker face in most situations—if I do say so myself—and I kept my lips zipped. There was a risk of him walking away, but since he'd been the one to raise the subject of the murdered man, I gambled that he had more to say.

"He had a pretty sweet motorbike. I went over to the store a few times to check it out. Tried to convince him to let me take it for a ride."

"How was that working out for you?"

Dylan grimaced and shot me a wry smile. "I'd made some progress."

"He let you touch it?"

He laughed. "Yeah."

"You're into motorbikes?"

"Totally." He broke eye contact to brush crumbs off the crease of his ironed-to-perfection trousers.

"What sort of bike is it?"

The boy's forehead collapsed into thoughtful furrows. "Ah. A Harley." His voice rose on the 'ley,' as if he were asking a question.

"Yeah. It's a Harley," he repeated with more confidence. "Mint condition."

Everyone I knew who harbored a lust for anything with wheels would offer more than a brand name when asked about the object of their desire. They'd bombard you with so much detail, trivia, and history of that particular model that your eyes would glaze over within seconds.

I didn't believe Dylan Werth was telling the truth about his love of motorbikes. Or his visits to Lucas Kerr.

But before I could figure out a way to dig a little deeper into his relationship with the dead man, someone blasted an air horn beside me.

Spinning around—and nearly falling on my butt in the process—I saw nothing but weather-worn gravestones and the depressed angel. Another vicious honk sounded. My gaze dropped to the base of the angel monument and the biggest, meanest bird I'd ever seen.

Its tail feathers quivering, it dipped its snake-like neck in our direction.

"What is *that*?" I asked Dylan out of the corner of my mouth, not daring to take my eyes off the critter's sharp-looking beak.

"It's Reggie," Dylan said. "The vicar's pet goose."

Shows you how long it had been since I'd last attended

church. I knew nothing about Peter Salmon's soft spot for feathered demons. "Is it going to attack us?"

I calculated how fast I could run and divided the answer by how much my restrictive dress and pretty-but-useless heels would handicap me.

"Not if we feed him." Dylan's clothes rustled as he clambered to his feet. "I usually save him some cake, but today you distracted me, and I ate his share."

Oops, my bad. Now we had a killer Godfather in avian form wanting to exact payment.

"I have Tic Tacs in my purse," I said.

In case Reggie was partial to minty-fresh breath.

"Tic Tacs will only make him mad," said a voice from the other side of the wall.

EIGHT

In slo-mo increments, I turned my head toward the owner of the voice.

Oliver Novak.

Beside his jeans-covered leg stood a panting, fluffy white cloud with a black nose and a pink harness around its body.

Both were grinning.

Glad I could provide free entertainment to the locals.

"This is much more to his liking." He held up the remains of a croissant.

I narrowed my eyes at him, careful not to make any sudden moves that the demon goose might interpret as aggressive. "How much do you want for it?"

The white fluffball tilted its head up at the man who held the pink leash. Awaiting his answer.

Oliver's grin expanded. "Just a replacement breakfast pastry at your convenience."

Seemed fair. "I'll agree to that."

Reggie let out an extended *hooooonk*. Seemed someone was all out of patience.

Oliver tossed the chunk of croissant to the far right of where Dylan and I stood frozen. Wings beating, the goose waddled double time in that direction. Did Reggie enjoy his ill-gotten gains? No idea. I toed off my impractical shoes and hightailed it out of the cemetery, hot on Dylan's heels. After hastily exchanged "Byes," Dylan and I went our separate ways. Him to hunt down his parents, me as far away from the vicar and his bad-tempered fowl as possible.

At the corner of the church wall, where it finished on Beach Street, Oliver and the white ball of fur waited for me. At least, I assumed they were waiting for me.

"Thanks for your sacrifice." I drew up alongside them and stuffed my grass-stained feet back into my shoes, which the dog promptly set about sniffing. "If I'm not mistaken, that was a croissant from Disco's."

"It was. And you're welcome." He clicked his tongue, and the fluffball ignored him, continuing to investigate my shoes.

I hoped Kit hadn't peed in them sometime in the recent past. "I kind of inherited my nana's two cats. They like to hide in my closet and sleep all over my shoes. She must be able to smell them."

Because a guy who looked tough enough to hold his own in a street brawl was interested in A: how many cats I'd inherited, and B: where I kept my footwear.

Then again, he was walking the doggy equivalent of a powder-puff.

"She's a he," Oliver said. "Meet Maki, the Japanese Spitz."

We crossed the street, me pressing my lips together to hold in a snicker. "Maki, as in sushi rolls?

"Uh-huh." His eyebrow quirked up, daring me to laugh.

"He's my neighbor's dog. I walk Maki for her because she can't."

Feeling bad for mentally making fun of the pup, I crouched to let him sniff my fingers before scratching between his cute fuzzy ears. I also felt a warm fuzzy at Oliver's kindness toward an elderly neighbor.

"You're very, very sweet." Maki licked my wrist in agreement, and I stood.

That compliment might have included Maki's dog-walker—not that I was about to admit it.

"Appearances can be deceiving," Oliver said as Maki, having lost interest in my shoes, yipped and trotted as far away from us as his leash would allow. "See you around." He and the fluffball continued down Beach Street.

On the short walk back to Unraveled, my mind gnawed over my conversation with the Werth kid. Was Dylan what he appeared to be—a seventeen-year-old boy who admired a newcomer's motorbike and still went to church with his parents? Or was he a seventeen-year-old boy who deceived his parents by sneaking out at night? The two were both normal teenage behaviors.

With a shake of my head, I scooped up Kit, who was sunning himself on a brick wall six houses away from home. Expecting a teenager to remain in his room was about as futile as expecting a cat to stay in its own yard. Just like my black kitties, teenagers lived to roam. Kit purred loudly in my ear as I stroked his soft fur and continued down the street.

If only people were as uncomplicated as cats.

THE NEXT MORNING, I prepared to take one for the team by going to my ten o'clock appointment at Discovery Dental Surgery. An email appointment had arrived in my inbox first thing this morning, thanks to a cancellation. Show me a person who doesn't have a little lead in their shoes as they walk into a dentist's, and I'll show you a liar. With my *it's okay; I'm okay* smile fixed in place, I made my way into the surgery's reception, where Jennifer Werth sat behind the desk.

Jennifer was probably the only female alive over the age of twelve who could pull off the headband look. Today's band, white with tiny turquoise flowers, perfectly complemented her white silk blouse. Come to think of it, Jennifer was probably the only female alive who could wear white silk without fear of dribbling coffee down the front or underarm stains appearing in the summer heat. White was not a color that appeared in my closet, mainly because black hides a multitude of sins.

"Tessa, isn't it?" Jennifer said before I could announce myself.

"Yes. From across the road."

As her plum-slicked lips puckered, I couldn't help taking a mental snapshot of her lipstick color to compare with the smears on Lucas's cup. It didn't appear to be a match.

"We were so sorry to hear about Nana Dee-Dee, but wasn't it a lovely send-off the ladies of Saint Barnabas gave her?"

"Lovely," I agreed.

Though how an abundance of club sandwiches, cakes, and slices, plus the requisite funeral refreshment, sausage rolls, could take the sting out of the worst day of the Wakefields' lives, I had no idea.

"And it was so *lovely* to see you at church yesterday."

If the woman's fake smile grew any brighter, I'd need sunblock. However, if I got in first, I might dodge what was likely to be an invitation to join a women's bible study group...

"I had a chat with your Dylan after the service," I blurted.

Maybe it was my imagination, but her smile seemed to dial down a notch. She gave an airy chuckle, flicking her hand as if swatting a fly. "Goodness! Did you manage to get more than a few grunts out of him?"

"A little. He mentioned his interest in motorbikes."

Jennifer's nose crinkled. "Motorbikes? That doesn't sound like Dylan. He's always on about carbon emissions and global warming. He's mad on environmental stuff, just like my sister. That's why he's applying to study law at the University of Canterbury next year. Wants to be an 'environmental lawyer.'" She used two fingers of each hand to punctuate this and rolled her eyes. But her tone was all proud mama bear.

"That's impressive. He must be gearing up to work extremely hard during his final year," I said.

"Dylan gets such good grades in school. Nose to the grindstone—he's always got a book in his hands."

The door into reception flew open, and Beth Chadwick stomped out, closely followed by the hulking white-shirted shape of the dentist. Who appeared to be making a valiant attempt to keep a grin hidden under his beard.

Without acknowledging me, Beth turned her steely gaze on Jennifer. "I'd wring his scrawny neck if I were fast enough to catch him. And you can tell the vicar I said so at the next prayer meeting, because I won't be there." Beth angled both double chins upward in defiance. "I refuse to step foot on hallowed ground until he gets rid of that...that disgusting, pooping *thing*."

Pausing, probably to breathe since her cheeks had flushed chili-pepper red, she must have caught sight of me. Standing there with my jaw about to hit the floor. I snapped it shut. "Do you mean Reggie, the goose?"

Beth harrumphed. "Feathered devil." She tapped the side of her nose. "Satan was once an angel with wings, did you know that? Reggie's worse. I was cleaning the church after the service yesterday when that menace somehow got inside. He snuck up behind me in the ladies' lavatory and let out an almighty squawk. I got such a fright; my bottom dentures flew out and went straight into the loo. I was so panicked, I flushed!"

"Oh, my." With the effort of not exploding into ill-timed giggles, my voice came out all reedy. "How terrible."

Perhaps mistaking my breathlessness for concern, Beth patted my arm. "Don't you worry, dear. I'll be passing on the bill for a replacement to Saint Barnabas."

Brian cleared this throat and caught my eye. "If you'd like to come through?"

I could think of nothing I'd like less. As I slunk past the dentist's formidable girth, it struck me that a possible murderer was about to poke sharp objects into my mouth.

Worst. Dentistry. Experience. *Ever*.

"NERVOUS?" Brian said as I made like a chameleon and attempted to disappear into the pasty-beige patient chair.

"Is it that obvious?" I white-knuckled the single armrest, my jaw already aching from the effort of clamping it shut.

The dentist's shoes squeaked on the linoleum as he

walked behind me and out of my line of sight, thanks to me being helpless in a chair designed by sadists and found comfortable only by masochists. Really, whoever built them should have had the foresight to include lockable straps to prevent people like me fleeing out the door.

I craned my neck, but to no avail. Seriously, what was he doing back there?

Inhaling what I hoped would be a calming breath, I reminded myself why I must suffer those sharp instruments.

"Your wife mentioned Dylan wants to study law next year."

A grunt from behind me. "If he works harder. He'd rather game his days away than study or get a summer job. The boy needs to develop some kind of work ethic before he takes off to university. It's crucial he doesn't ruin his chances at a successful career."

Pressure much? But I latched onto his earlier statement. "A summer job, like at Hanburys? Or the pop-up store?"

Another grunt followed by a shoe squeak as Brian reappeared. "Just as well he didn't get a job there, considering." He shook out a paper bib and deftly fastened it around my neck. "Tragic business."

"Yeah." I slid him a sideways glance as he leaned the other way to retrieve a pair of dark-lensed sunglasses from his tray of lethal weapons. Had Dylan applied for a job with Lucas? Is that why he'd hung around the store?

Brian passed me the glasses, and I slid them on while he adjusted the torture chamber's spotlight onto my face.

"Heard the cops questioned Sean at the Napier station on Saturday," he said.

"Just dotting their i's and crossing their t's. Standard procedure." I had no idea if this was true or not.

A scary-looking metal instrument appeared above my nose, followed by the bushy eyebrows of the dentist. "Let's have a look."

Cue for me to open my mouth; I did so with much trepidation.

Pick, pick, pick went the miniature hook as it worked around my back teeth. I clenched my hands into fists to keep myself from knocking the tool straight across the room.

"I'm sure your brother wasn't involved."

"Ee-osn't," I replied.

Brian's nose filled my vision. The man needed to invest in a hair trimmer. Top left molars now, pick-pick-pick.

"Ee ott on ell if ookas."

"He got on well with Lucas?" Brian translated, obviously fluent in wide-open-mouthed-English.

"Uh-uh."

Nasal hairs rippled as Brian wrinkled his nose. "Not to speak ill and all that, but the man was scum. Your brother has poor taste in friends." After picking around to my top right molars, he finally removed the instrument from my mouth.

My jaw creaked shut in relief. "Lucas was his boss; they weren't friends. Neither were you and he, or so I believe."

I couldn't see the dentist's face, but the absolute stillness in the room told me he'd heard every word. He hissed out a breath. "A lot of people in this town didn't like him."

"I don't think dislike was the reason Lucas turned up dead with a knife sticking out of his back."

"Maybe the drugs?" Brian made a sucking sound like he was mashing his tongue against his teeth. "Seems to me someone did Cape Discovery a favor by taking that dirtbag out of the picture."

He turned away, and rattling sounds came from his instrument tray. When he leaned back over me, he held in his meaty fist what I assumed was the dreaded drill.

"We'll give your pearly whites a quick polish, hmm?" he said.

I'm not ashamed to say tears of relief sprang from my eyes under the dark sunglasses. Polishing I could cope with. I nodded—not that he appeared to be waiting for permission, as the polisher whizzed to life—and obediently opened wide.

But before the minty paste could touch my teeth, I blurted out, "I think someone killed Lucas for more personal reasons."

The polisher abruptly stopped, and Brian's caterpillar eyebrows arrowed down. "Like what?"

"A woman," I said. "Maybe a jealous boyfriend...or husband." I was thankful for the sunglasses as the dentist's gaze grew flinty.

"What are you implying?"

"Just that you might have had an issue with the way Lucas behaved toward your wife."

"And because I look like some thug who manhandles drunks out of a nightclub instead of a dentist, you assume I bashed his head in?"

I blinked up at him. Now that he mentioned it, he did look more like a bouncer than a dentist. It wouldn't have taken much effort on his part to overpower Lucas, a much smaller man.

The buzzing started again. "Open, please."

I obeyed, and minty freshness assaulted my nose. As the polisher traversed my teeth, I watched the dentist watching me.

"On the night of the murder," he said briskly, "I was home with my wife and stepson. After dinner, we all went for a walk along the beach. Back home, we watched a movie together, then Dylan and I played a few games on his PlayStation before we all went to bed."

"An or ife?"

"And my wife?" His giant shoulders lifted in a shrug. "I overreacted to a bit of harmless flirting. We talked it out—or rather, she talked; I agreed I'd overreacted and anything and everything was my fault..." He gave me a henpecked smile to show that although he looked as if he could extract teeth from a great white without fear, he was scared of his five-foot-two wife and was, therefore, harmless. "And that was the end of that."

As the buzzing polisher was now so far back in my mouth that I feared swallowing it, I gave him a thumbs up to show I believed him. Though I wasn't sure I really did.

The dentist raised the chair to the upright position and instructed me to rinse and spit.

I swirled the pale blue rinse around my gritty, minty mouth.

"If you're looking for someone who had it in for Lucas, you should talk to Dylan's school principal."

The liquid splattered out of me, staining blue droplets around the basin. I swiveled abruptly, my feet tumbling off the chair to hit the floor. "You mean Isabel Burton?"

"Dylan saw her waiting out the back of the store a few times."

"That's hardly evidence she *had it in* for Lucas. She could've been waiting for Sean." A perfectly reasonable assumption, except I somehow doubted Isabel and my brother had anything in common.

No. If Isabel had hung around outside the store, she must have been waiting for the owner, not Sean.

I replayed last Thursday night's knitting group discussion when Lucas's name had cropped up. What had Isabel said? She'd asked Skye whether Lucas had done or said anything inappropriate. And she'd blushed.

"Not according to Dylan." Brian's voice dropped to a conspirator's level. "Last year, before school finished for the term, Dylan was meeting with Ms. Burton about a fundraising campaign he and some other students were organizing. She was called out of the meeting for a moment and left her phone on the desk. He said he couldn't help but see Lucas's name flash up on the screen with a brief, but, ah, personal message."

I didn't want to ask, but curiosity compelled me. "What did it say?"

Brian shook his head. "Dylan was too embarrassed to repeat it. We stumbled onto the perils of sexting by accident, and I think he was already regretting telling me that much. He just said it was majorly NSFW."

Not suitable for work. Huh.

So, Isabel and Lucas. Huh, again.

"You might want to..." Brian touched his chin. "With the bib."

Oh, yeah. Splash back and drool. I dabbed my lips and chin with the paper bib. It came away stained with pale blue splotches. Sophistication personified, that was me. I dumped the sunglasses on the armrest and slid off the chair.

"Your teeth are in tip-top condition," he said, as if this were a normal checkup. "I'll have Jennifer set up an appointment reminder for next year."

"Thanks." I snatched up my purse from beside the torture chair and fled.

Jennifer was on the phone when I approached her desk to pay. She covered the mouthpiece. "I'll send Brian's bill out to you. He knows where you live." With a dismissive wave, she returned to her call.

I slunk out of the surgery, wondering if her words were actually a thinly veiled threat.

NINE

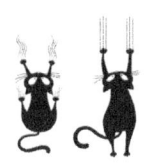

Business tended to be brisk on Monday mornings, with customers who'd knitted or crocheted up a storm during the weekend replenishing their yarn stashes. This Monday morning was even busier than usual, with every town gossip wanting my advice on one kind of yarn or another...as an excuse to vicariously experience my *gruesome discovery*.

Harry and I shifted more stock in eight hours than we had over the entire past month. Seemed murder made for good business. And the sign-up sheet for an after-hours class for beginners—which had stubbornly remained blank after I pinned it to the store's noticeboard two weeks ago—was now filled with names. Apparently, a quick overview of Friday morning's events had only whetted the scandalmongers' appetites.

A number of our Serial Knitter and Happy Hooker regulars called into the store and volunteered to help with tomorrow night's first lesson. Generous, but altruism wasn't the main reason for this sudden interest in teaching others yarn crafts at Nana Dee-Dee's store.

I still thought of Unraveled as my nana's. It wasn't that I hadn't had fun working there with Harry these past few months. I'd enjoyed the slower small-town pace and easy companionship of my granddad immensely. And it wasn't that Harry was territorial over how I managed Unraveled. He was all for my ideas of implementing an online shopping option and a social media presence. I just didn't know whether I, a mundane eight-ply, could be knitted into the brightly colored, sparkly community around me without forming holes and dropped stitches in the smooth stockinette that was Cape Discovery.

How was that for a creative metaphor?

Nana Dee-Dee would have told me to get over myself.

I sank into one of the two armchairs and picked up another of my new initiatives from the basket beside it: a sample square to be added to the growing pile of customer-created ones then sewn into charity rugs. After stroking my fingertips over the piece's soft bumps, I began knitting another row of seed stitch someone else had started. As the repetitive knit one, purl one worked its magic, the tension tightening my spine seeped out into the needles and got lost in the motion.

The bell above Unraveled's door tinkled, and I glanced up as Isabel stepped inside. Just the person I wanted to see. And since she hadn't yet spotted me, I took the opportunity to really *see* her. Not as the high school principal or as a semi-regular customer, but as a woman.

And a potential killer.

Although uncomfortable analyzing her attractiveness to the opposite sex, even in the privacy of my mind, if what Brian Werth said was true...

Physically, Isabel was a little taller than me and heavier

through the waist and hips, which she tried to disguise with tops that skimmed over those areas and instead highlighted her other assets. Two in particular that some men would consider irresistible. As she was growing her shoulder-length brown hair out of an unfortunate haircut—her words, not mine—she kept it off her roundish face with a bandana tied rakishly in a make-do hairband. In my opinion, her unremarkable face became pretty when she smiled, which she didn't often do. If I had to describe what I knew of her personality in one word, it would be...earnest.

Sparrow-like, her gaze darted around the shop and finally landed on me. "There you are. I thought you must've abandoned your post from sheer exhaustion."

"It's been a busy morning. I needed a break." I set the needles back in the basket—a dozen new rows added to the square—and smiled. "Can I help you with something?"

"I thought it was about time I overcame my fear of double-pointed needles and tackled a pair of socks. What can you tempt me with?"

We spent the next fifteen minutes in pleasant discussion about patterns, yarn, and the terrifying-at-first double-pointed needles. Proud of my budding salesperson skills, I easily talked her into two different sock patterns, top-of-the-line needles, plus two lovely hand-dyed hanks of wool-blend yarn from a local supplier. While she debated with herself over color choice—and there were many—Kit sashayed into the store and twined around my ankles.

I scooped him up and cuddled him on his back, giving him a belly scratch at the same time. Pearl would've torn my hand to shreds at the indignity of the position, but Kit purred at an ear-splitting decibel.

"Oh, look at him," Isabel cooed. She shoved the

turquoise yarn back on the shelf and dug around in her purse until she found her small container of cat treats. "Here you are, you beautiful boy." She offered him a treat, and he gently cupped her fingers with his front paws as he accepted it.

Kit had no issues with exploiting the cuteness factor for his own gains. Sure enough, she offered him a second treat. After he'd crunched that down, I set him on his feet.

"That's enough for you, chunky monkey," I said as he swished his tail in annoyance at his plans being thwarted. "Your fangs will fall out."

A not-so-subtle lead into the subject of Dylan Werth.

"Oh, no," Isabel said with utter seriousness. "There's no sugar in these."

"I just had a dental checkup this morning. Guess I'm a little paranoid."

Isabel returned the treats to her bag, but before she could resume poring over yarn colors, I said, "Their son goes to your school, doesn't he? I hear he's doing very well academically."

Her hand froze halfway to the shelf. "Who told you that? Dylan?"

"His mother."

"Ah. Parents." She didn't roll her eyes, but the eye-roll was in the tone of her voice. "Dylan's exam results won't be out for a couple of days, but if his derived grade exam results are anything to go by... He might want to reconsider university is all I'll say." Her lips sucked in for a moment. "I shouldn't have said that. It was most unprofessional of me."

"Do you know Dylan well?"

"No more than I know any of our seniors. He's a good student—well, up until the halfway through last year, anyway. He was a shoo-in for ahead prefect role this year, but after our last meeting..."

"Something happened at your last meeting?" I prompted.

She exhaled loudly through her nose; her jaw clenched tight. "He didn't seem himself. He was...off, somehow."

Was that before or after he'd seen the inappropriate message on her phone? I risked losing a loyal customer by confronting Isabel, but weighted against my brother's future, there seemed no other option.

"Because he found out about your relationship with Lucas Kerr?"

Her eyes bugged open. "Pardon?"

"You and Lucas. He saw a message on your phone while you were out of the room."

Isabel's face had paled, except for two red splotches on her cheekbones. "He must've misunderstood. Lucas and I were not in a relationship."

"You weren't romantically involved?"

"Romantic?" She got a pinched look on her face. "No, I wouldn't say romantic. We flirted back and forth on a couple of occasions when I was in his store. Lucas was a handsome man, and I was flattered by the attention."

I nodded in what I hoped was an encouraging but non-judgmental way.

"But whatever that young man *thought* he saw on my phone, I'd take with a grain of salt."

"It didn't go further than that?" I pressed. "You never went to the store after hours or to his RV?"

Isabel visibly stiffened, her shoulders thrusting back. "Absolutely not. And I don't like what you're suggesting. How could you believe I had something to do with that man's tragic demise?" With a wince, she clapped a hand to her lower back, muttering about her sciatica.

Lucas had been relegated to 'that man' within the space of a few seconds. A deliberate ploy to psychologically distance herself from someone she'd been attracted to? Call me suspicious, but was flirting really all there'd been between them?

"Come sit down." I guided her to the armchair I'd vacated.

Isabel gingerly lowered herself into the seat, hugging her purse close to her stomach. "Honestly, if you're trying to do the police's job for them, I'd recommend you ask Edward Hanbury about the real reason he hated Lucas."

I plopped into the second armchair and crossed my legs. "I thought it was professional rivalry. Lucas undercutting Ed's prices."

Isabel let out a lip-curling *pffft*. "That's what he'd trumpet about to anyone who'd listen. It's a reason, but it's not the *real* reason."

She lowered her voice—although we were now alone in the store. Apart from Kit, who'd found a stray sunbeam and was licking his furry hindquarters. "Last year, I was caught out by a sciatica attack outside the pop-up store, so I stopped to rest against the wall until it passed. Lucas and Ed were out the back of the store, at the end of the driveway. They didn't appear to notice me, probably because they were deep in a heated discussion. Ed looked as if he wanted to take a swing at Lucas but didn't quite dare. Lucas said, 'If you don't want your wife finding out about your checkout chick on the side, you'll do as I ask.'"

"Ed's having an affair?"

"Sure sounded that way."

"Donna will be devastated." My heartstrings knotted

with sympathy. "They've just celebrated their twenty-fifth wedding anniversary."

"Men are dogs," Isabel said. "The lot of 'em."

While I didn't agree with her generalization, there were certainly a few who fit that description. Jared immediately sprang to mind. But I wasn't going to waste a second dwelling on his spineless lack of character, not as I recalled the last part of Isabel's story.

"Lucas was blackmailing Ed. What did he want him to do?"

"A lawnmower started up somewhere behind the shop, and I missed what they said next." Her hand slipped between her hip and the armchair, and she winced. "Despite the pain, I didn't want to be caught eavesdropping, so I hobbled away as fast as I could."

By this time, Isabel had released her death grip on her purse, perhaps assuming she'd successfully diverted my busybody attention elsewhere. "You know, I think I'll go for the carnation pink, soft violet, and primrose yellow. They're all such pretty colors; I just can't choose one. Could you ring those up for me?"

"Certainly."

I made my way over to the fingering weight yarn and selected the right shades. The soft and squishy yarn would knit up into a snuggly pair of socks. As I bagged Isabel's purchases, she slowly made her way to the service counter.

"My guess is Ed's sleeping with Bianca or Monique," she said. "It's a small world. I taught Monique math about five years ago." Her nose crinkled. "The girl can't function without a cash register doing all the work for her."

With a perfunctory smile, I handed over the bag. "Math was never my strong suit either."

"Can't imagine what she and Ed have in common, given

that he's all about the numbers." She tucked the bag under her arm. "I'll see you on Thursday night. Hopefully, someone will be able to show me how to cast on with these metal toothpicks."

Isabel walked to the door, her gait easier and apparently pain free. She opened the door and hesitated before turning back to me with a grim chuckle. "Ed's such a tightwad. It really must've burned his britches having to fork over his hard-earned cash. Have to say, it serves him right."

Then with a wink, she left, Pearl slipping inside as the door swung closed behind her. Tail waving at the sky, she trotted over to greet her brother with a nose kiss before the two of them sprawled out, sharing the afternoon sunbeam.

I replayed our conversation. Could Ed's affair have anything to do with Lucas's murder? How much had Ed paid to keep his blackmailer silent? Was money even what the blackmailer was after? And more importantly, if it wasn't, what might Ed have done to shut his blackmailer up?

Permanently.

AS HARRY WAS A FORMER COP, my inability to remain patient on a stakeout must have come from a different part of the gene pool.

After Isabel's earlier revelations, I found myself skulking around outside the Hanburys' house at nine thirty that night. Helpfully, to counterbalance my below-par stakeout skills, the Hanburys owned a McMansion on the waterfront. I was able to comfortably hide in plain sight on a conveniently placed public bench facing the ocean. Just another holidaymaker taking in the view of a full moon glimmering on the softly pleated waves as they hissed ashore.

There was also enough of a nip in the air that a hooded sweatshirt didn't look out of place. That sounds way cooler than the reality. Rather than a black ninja hoodie, my only hooded sweatshirt was pastel pink, complete with pointed cat ears sewn onto the hood and embroidered whiskers on the kangaroo-style pocket. A joke gift from Mum a couple of birthdays ago. But the joke was on her because I adored it.

As the minutes ticked by with no sign of Ed and Winnie stepping out for their nightly walkies, I kept myself amused by inventing superhero names.

Captain Feline.
Secret Agent Dumb-Luck.
Super-Knitty Ninja Kitty.

Before I could invent a superhero movie franchise that would be laughed out of Hollywood, an outside security light turned on at the Hanburys. As I flicked up my cat ears hood, Ed and Winnie ambled toward Cape Street. They didn't turn but instead continued on along the waterfront, heading in the direction of Cape Discovery's campground.

Where Lucas Kerr's RV had been parked until the police removed it as evidence.

Aha!

With my sneaky sneakers on, I tailed the two perps. Neither appeared to be aware of being followed in catlike-stealth mode.

Confession: I was enjoying the heck out of this impromptu nighttime escapade.

In my previous life—commute for an hour, work, commute an hour home again to a man who grew more distant daily, rinse, and repeat—spontaneity didn't exist. Every day, week, month fitted neatly into the dull routine

Jared had carved out for us. I'd sleepwalked through most of my twenties. And even worse, I hadn't wanted anyone to wake me because my reality had been too pathetically lonely to bear.

So, being out at night with a briny breeze whispering around me and the golden glow of streetlights competing with moonlight...revived my childhood dreams of adventure. Of course, at nine, my idea of adventure was more digging up Dad's herb garden, searching for buried treasure than tailing a middle-aged man and his elderly Labrador.

I kept what I figured was a safe distance between Ed and myself as he made a right turn into Beach Street. When Winnie stopped to do her thing on a grass verge in front of someone's house, I tucked myself into a hedge-lined driveway. My estimation of Ed's character plummeted even further when he continued along the street rather than picking up after his dog.

Ick.

As Ed's steps slowed, I crouched behind a conveniently planted decorative shrub. He performed a quick three-sixty scan of the street before tugging Winnie into a driveway opposite the campground's far corner. From the upstairs windows, whoever lived in the nondescript weatherboard house would have a perfect view of the vehicles parked behind the campground's privacy fence.

I crept closer, hoping to catch a glimpse of whoever he was visiting at this late hour. Luck of the ninjas favored me. Ed stood under a security light in the house's open doorway, deep in a stage-whispered discussion with a woman. I couldn't see much of her other than the bottom of a bathrobe and fluffy slippers peeping out from between Ed's hands-on-hips stance.

Hunched over awkwardly behind her neighbor's white

picket fence, I was too far away to eavesdrop. If I duck-walked along behind the rose bushes spilling over a stone boundary wall, I could scoot across the driveway to the relative safety of a massive pillar. That would put the pair in my direct line of sight—and I'd be close enough to see and hear them.

The question was, could I traverse the exposed width of driveway without them seeing or hearing *me*?

Well, I was here already. *No guts, no glory.*

Making it to the end of the roses was a workout for my thighs and glutes, but hearing no shouts of alarm, I figured I was halfway home. Until I spotted a dog-shaped lump collapsed on the paving stones.

Winnie.

Taking a power nap while her owner was otherwise occupied. And her owner's mouth and hands were definitely otherwise occupied with the woman in the bathrobe.

Double ick.

But a perfect opportunity for me to scurry across the driveway. I would have made it too, if it weren't for the dog letting out an enormous fart in her sleep. After waking herself up with it, she barked to warn everyone around her.

The snogging duo sprang apart like teenagers busted by a parent, and Ed whirled around, witnessing my feet's sudden propensity to stick to the paving stones. Caught dead center of the driveway.

Oops.

As I saw it, there were only two ways to handle this. A: run like Mr. Darcy was waiting for me at an imaginary finish line. Or B: assume the moral high ground and go on the offensive.

I now had a better view of whose throat Ed had his tongue down mere seconds ago. It wasn't, as Isabel suspected, either of his two single staff members: Bianca and Monique. It was the store's assistant manager, Sharon White. Sharon, who was married to Andie, an affable truck driver who drove big rigs up and down the country.

Decision made, I ninja-jumped onto the moral high ground.

TEN

Throwing back my hood, I gave Sharon and Ed the kind of steely *don't even think about lying to me* glare I'd once used to silence even the unruliest teenagers in the school halls.

"Not fussy about whether or not the lady has a ring on her finger, huh, Hanbury? Your hypocrisy knows no bounds."

Ed spluttered, his face glowing like he'd squirreled hot embers in his cheeks. "It's not what it looks like."

"Puh-lease." I folded my arms and deliberately shifted my gaze beyond his left shoulder. "Perks of the job, Sharon?"

At least she had the decency to blush and lower her gaze.

"Were you following me?" Ed stomped down the driveway, stabbing a finger in my direction. "How dare you."

I stood my ground, curious as to how far he'd push his angry indignation in front of a witness. Not an impartial witness, I reminded myself. My stomach gave a sideways roll. Would she lie and say I'd struck first if push came to shove? Of course she would.

"I'm not the only one who knows about your little indiscretion." I exaggeratedly touched a finger to the side of my chin and tilted my head. "Wait a second. One of the other people who knew is *dead*."

"I had nothing to do with that."

Winnie barked, as if backing up Ed's statement. *Sorry, doggo, you're also a biased witness.*

"So, on the night Lucas Kerr died, you were just walking your dog. Nothing else? No detour to the old butcher shop to bash your blackmailer's brains in?"

"How did you know he was blackmailing me?" As his cheeks turned an even brighter shade of crimson, his beady-eyed gaze zigzagged around me. "And keep your voice down."

The scuff of slippers on the ground behind him snagged my attention moments before Sharon latched limpet-tight onto Ed's arm. "He was with me that night, okay?"

"Busy evening for you, Ed. Anniversary dinner with your wife, nightcap with your mistress, a spot of murder on your way home."

Sharon's heavily mascaraed eyelashes were in serious danger of sticking together as she glared at me. "Are you thick or something? Ed didn't kill anyone. He didn't leave my place until nearly one in the morning. Wasn't Lucas already dead by then?"

Unfortunately, he was. But I wasn't quite ready to let Ed off the hook.

"How did he find out about you two?"

Ed and Sharon exchanged guilty glances.

"He saw us coming out of my delivery warehouse one night," he said. "I tried telling him Shaz and I were just stocktaking, but he laughed and said, 'Mum's the word.' A few days later, I received a threatening email."

"What did he want?"

"Space in my warehouse for one of his shipments." Ed curled his lip. "He didn't outright say drugs, but that's what he meant."

"And did you accept this shipment?"

Ed hung his head. "I had no choice, did I? Donna would take me to the cleaners if she found out about Shaz and me. It was only meant to be for a few days. A week max."

"Where's that shipment now?"

Sharon grimaced as she chewed on her lower lip. "The boxes are still in a corner of the warehouse. Ed was waiting for further instructions." She stared at me with puppy-dog eyes. "We don't know what to do! We can't go to the police. We can't flush the...*product* down the loo because Lucas isn't around to sell it. And if Lucas can't sell it, then his suppliers won't get paid"—her voice continued to climb to a pitch that caused Winnie to whine—"and if his suppliers don't get paid, they'll come looking for the product and eventually trace it to us."

In other words, plenty of reason for them to want Lucas gone. But permanently? What Sharon was saying made sense. If Ed was holding illegal substances as a result of blackmail, the last thing he'd want was to be stuck with that hot potato if his blackmailer vanished.

Or happened to be cracked over the head with a wine bottle and then stabbed.

Ed slipped an arm around Sharon's shoulders and squeezed. Her mouth snapped shut, and she blinked rapidly, sticky black lashes fluttering. "Anyway, you're barking up the wrong tree with Eddie. He couldn't hurt a fly."

Ed angled his head to look down his slightly hooked nose at me. "Who was gossiping about Shaz and me?"

"I'd rather not say."

He gritted his teeth. "Was it that Burton woman? I've noticed her smirking at me when she comes in for her groceries."

When I neither confirmed nor denied, he grimaced. "Figures she'd try to turn suspicion on me. She's the one who had the biggest bone to pick with the dearly departed Romeo. Hell hath no fury, or so they say."

"Isabel claims they weren't in a romantic relationship."

At this, Sharon snorted. "A woman doesn't key a man's RV late at night for no reason."

Well. That was news. "Isabel keyed Lucas's RV?"

"Shaz spotted her from the upstairs window. You get a good view of the campground's west corner from her bedroom. Anyway, there she was, bold as you please, walking the length of his camper and scratching up his fancy paint job. Probably didn't realize she was visible from over here."

"You're positive it was Isabel?"

"I've attended enough prize-givings with my nephews to recognize the school principal when I see her," Sharon snipped.

"You didn't report this vandalism?" I asked.

"I would've high-fived her if I'd seen her," he said. "And encouraged her to do the same to the other side of his RV—which is probably what she did on the night of Lucas's murder. Right before she, the woman scorned, killed him."

A preposterous suggestion... Wasn't it?

I shook my head as if that might rearrange this new information swirling around my brain into some semblance of order.

Ed must have interpreted my action as adamant denial of his statement, as his chest puffed out, and he huffed imperiously through his nose. "I'm not pulling accusations out of thin air, Ms. Wakefield. I just happened to be looking out the window that night, when a woman slipped out of the western gate and into that short dead-end side street—what's its name?"

"Weka Grove," Sharon helpfully provided.

"That's it. There's only the one streetlight on Weka—and it was out that night—but I caught a glimpse of her. I bet she'd been hoping to confront the man. And when petty vandalism didn't satisfy her, she tracked him down to his store, and...well. We all know how one bad decision can lead to another and then get completely out of hand."

Substantially shorter than Ed, Sharon didn't see his gaze twitch down to the top of her head. Not my problem if there was trouble brewing in their sordid little paradise.

"Did you see her face? Even though the streetlight was out?"

Frown grooves appeared on his forehead. "No. But it looked like her. Similar height, similar build. Dressed in the kind of outfit and high heels a woman wears to impress a man."

Chauvinistic, much?

But I didn't always agree with the expression 'looks like a duck, swims like a duck, quacks like a duck...' Sometimes things looked duckish but were actually geese who'd peck you in the butt for jumping to conclusions.

"Anything else you can tell me about the woman?"

Ed's mouth twisted. "Only that she stalked away from the campground at a fast clip. Like someone who's late for an appointment or been stood up on a date and is off to give the other person a talking-to."

A breeze, briny-scented and damp, blew up the street and crept down my neck. I shivered, deciding I had no desire to linger a moment longer in Ed Hanbury's presence. While I could scratch him off my list of potential murderers, I didn't like him at all. Stuffing my hands into my pockets, I half-turned toward the sidewalk.

"Are you going to tell my wife about this...conversation?"

He meant would I tell his wife about him playing hide-the-sausage with their assistant manager. I needed a hot shower and a brisk loofah to scrub the slime off my body. But I met Ed's gaze. "No."

His shoulders sagged in relief. They shouldn't have. Because I wasn't promising the same about the drugs sitting in his warehouse. No way would I risk those ending up in the community. Detective Mana was about to have more than a murder on his hands.

As I owed neither of them a polite goodbye, I abruptly spun away and crossed to the once again snoozing Winnie. Petting her head, I told her what a good girl she was, then hotfooted it in the direction of home.

On the way, I sifted through the new information I'd learned.

If it looks like a duck, swims like a duck, and quacks like a duck, then it probably is a duck.

Maybe. Or was I heading off on a wild goose chase?

THE BEGINNERS KNITTING class looked set to be an overnight success. So much so, I had to call a dozen people to let them know they were on a waiting list.

Since this was a new class, I could organize it how I

wanted. As much as I'd loved and admired Nana Dee-Dee, she and Harry were big softies. They hadn't had the heart to charge their Thursday night group for the privilege of Nana Dee-Dee's time, expertise, and refreshments.

I was about to shake things up.

Starting with rule number one: All materials used in class must be purchased at Unraveled. Fair's fair, right? When you go to a nice restaurant, you don't smuggle in BYO mac 'n' cheese under your jacket.

Which meant that when the fifteen beginners filed through Unraveled's door that evening, Harry was kept busy ringing up purchases. As well as the newbies, I'd invited Isabel and Beth to assist—with the incentive of store credit as payment. Why those two? Because Beth had an unerring talent for ferreting out nuggets of gossip. And Isabel? I wanted to watch her reaction to that gossip being flung around the room.

Jennifer Werth and her friend, who I recognized as one of the two lawyers from across the road, had signed up for the class. Then two unexpected attendees arrived: Sharon White and my mother. Figuring out Mum's agenda wasn't difficult. No one would dare bad-mouth Maggie's baby boy with her there. Sharon's motivation was trickier. She gave me a tight smile, saying she was taking her friend's spot for this week. Purportedly, to *take her mind off things*.

'Things' being the raid on Hanburys' warehouse in the early hours of this morning, and the discovery of thousands of dollars' worth of illicit substances. Courtesy of my anonymous tip-off to the Napier Police. Ed was apparently insisting he'd no idea what Lucas had stored in his warehouse; he'd simply been a helpful fellow store owner. I doubted the police had bought his story, but even though he was covering his own butt, at least he'd kept his wife and mistress out of it.

Once all the attendees had settled around the worktable with their purchased cotton yarn and suitable needles for making a beginner-friendly dishcloth, I divided them into two groups. The absolute newbies, who didn't know a knitting needle from a chopstick, were in one group, while the 'my nana/mum/auntie taught me when I was a kid, but I can't remembers' formed the other. I delegated the larger, second group to Beth and my mum, while Isabel and I took the baby beginners.

While demonstrating how to cast on and form a knit stitch, I kept a close eye on Sharon, who'd raised her hand to join our group. Not completely immune to the sight of her trembling fingers as she tried to make her needles obey, I steadied her shaking right hand so she could complete a stitch.

Her skin felt chilled as she winced a smile up at me. "You make it look easier than it is. Perhaps I'm not ready to take up a new hobby."

"Rubbish." Isabel, sitting two seats down, leaned forward in her chair and patted Sharon's elbow. "You'll get the hang of it. Just remember the rhyme Tessa taught you. In through the front door, once around the back, peek through the window, and off jumps Jack!"

Across the table, Beth gave an evil chuckle and bared her teeth—the old girl must have a spare set of falsies. "Or here's another: Stab him, strangle him, pull him down, dump his body. Doesn't rhyme, but it's rather apt, don't you think?"

Isabel sat back in her chair so fast it was a minor miracle she didn't give herself whiplash. There were a few snickers and some tongue-tutting around the table; however, Isabel's reaction interested me most. She had a complexion that usually turned her cheeks rosy in a warm environment, but I watched as that color drained to pasty splotches. Her fingers gripped the needles so tightly I was glad I'd provided her with a metal set instead of plastic or bamboo.

"That's a little off-color, Beth." Under today's mustard-yellow beanie, Harry's forehead crumpled in concern.

"Too soon?" Beth's shark-like smile didn't waver. "I'm just saying what everyone else is thinking."

She wasn't wrong.

I'd noticed some of the newbies sneaking curious glances at my mother, myself, and Sharon, and a few lowered heads and hushed conversations happening below the laughter and griping of learning a new skill.

"I wasn't thinking about Mr. Kerr." The lawyer, whose name I now remembered was Kaye, thanks to the 'KAYEnne pepper' color of her hair, made a stabbing motion with one of her needles and managed to drop at least three stitches. "May he rot in jail for peddling drugs to children. No, as a professional, I just find it so shocking that one of our town's prominent citizens is mixed up in all of that."

Muttered comments of 'such a terrible thing,' 'the gall,' and 'unforgivable behavior' rippled around the room. My cynical side wondered if Kaye was planning to campaign for Ed's position in DOPE.

Kaye turned her attention to where Sharon sat next to my granddad, shrinking into her chair as if she wanted to slither under the table. "You and the staff must still be in shock at what's happened."

"Yes, we are. Shocked," Sharon parroted in a reedy, breathless voice.

Beth's needles resumed clicking at light speed, working

on the dishcloth she was meant to be demonstrating to her students instead of knitting herself. "Goes to show, you never really know someone, even when you work such long hours with them."

She gave Sharon a bland stare over the rims of her reading glasses, and I could almost hear the hamster-wheel whirr of her brain as she tried to figure out just how well this Hanburys' employee knew her boss.

"His poor wife," Jennifer said. "Was she aware of what he was up to, do you think?"

She directed the comment to Beth, who seemed to be shaping up as the group's oracle on all things scandalous.

Sharon wobbled to her feet. "Excuse me. Where's the bathroom?"

Harry stood and rested a reassuring hand on her shoulder. "I'll show you, love. Come with me." My granddad shot me an indecipherable look as he guided Sharon out of the room.

The second they left the workroom, Beth pounced. "It's all connected. The warehouse raid, the drugs found in the old butcher shop, and Lucas Kerr's murder. It must be." Her needles clicked even faster. Soon there would be nothing left for her students to complete.

"Ed and Lucas were drug-dealing partners, but something went wrong, and Ed offed him," Beth continued. "Isn't that the likeliest scenario, Tessa? Aren't you carrying out your own investigation?"

"Um." Not the slickest of responses, but she'd caught me off guard.

A roomful of curious gazes swiveled toward me, including my mother's. With that irritating maternal mind-meld that women seem to have with their daughters, I sensed her willing me to agree with Beth's assessment of

Ed's guilt. *Do it for your brother*, her pinched lips and pleading eyes seemed to say.

"I wouldn't say I was investigating Lucas's death. That's the police's job." Stalling for time, I admit it.

"Pigs. More interested in hassling innocent protesters than tracking down murderers," Nadia snapped. Nadia, an early twenty-something student, had declared she was learning to knit so she could yarn bomb the 'oppressive patriarchal' university she attended.

Good luck to her. She'd probably leave knitted versions of the male anatomy on all the campus doorknobs.

"But you are unofficially trying to discover who the killer is in this community?" Beth insisted. "Though we don't know for sure that it *is* someone from Discovery."

Jennifer spoke up before I could. "In my opinion, it's more likely another drug dealer from Napier was involved. Maybe some sort of turf war with a rival gang."

Nods and murmurs of agreement greeted her statement. No one in this sleepy town wanted to think their neighbor, friend, or grocery store owner could be a killer. But I knew details that the police hadn't released to the general public. Such as, what self-respecting drug lord would crack his victim over the head with a wine bottle instead of the easier bullet to the brain? Guess it wasn't completely out of the question, but a gang hit didn't explain the need for a coroner's toxicology report.

I slid my hand into the pocket of my pants and curled my fingers around the leprechaun pin I'd started carrying with me. Somehow, Lucas's death felt more personal than a simple execution.

"But what if it *was* someone from Discovery?" Isabel said. "What if they get away with cold-blooded murder, and we're left with a killer in our midst?"

Jennifer sighed. "In that event, maybe the guilty person will be overcome with remorse. They could suffer a crisis of conscience and choose the easy way out rather than face serious prison time."

Kaye snorted. "Prison, where he could join another gang and learn even more nefarious skills? And *serious* prison time? What a joke."

A number of *why the justice system is flawed* conversations sprang up.

Taking a deep breath to steady my racing pulse, I knocked on the tabletop to gain everyone's attention. "Whoever killed Lucas has opened a crack in Cape Discovery," I said. "And we all have to choose whether we'll allow that crack to widen and drive this community apart with rumors and accusations, or..." I paused for effect, making steady eye contact with each person in the room. "Or whether we mend that crack by sticking together and trusting that justice will be served."

More nods and murmurs of agreement, and this time, it was as if the ill-feeling evaporated from the room. Except for the thundercloud forming over Beth's perfectly coifed curls.

With a huff, she shoved her needles and yarn into the lap of the woman next to her. "Trust in justice? How? By sitting on our *be*-hinds and knitting dishcloths? Who's to say some other drug lord won't turn up to take Lucas's place and set up his headquarters in town?"

Harry returned to his spot at the table, but instead of taking a seat, he switched his former-cop stare on Beth until her mouth snapped shut. "If that happens, the town council will recruit you to yarn bomb said headquarters. Until then, we let the police do their jobs and get back to sitting on our *be*-hinds."

"Right then," I said in the most enthusiastic tone I could muster. "Who's ready to mix things up and conquer the purl stitch?"

EXHAUSTION CAME in blurry waves as I ushered the last student out of Unraveled at ten. Darkness had spread its tentacles through town, but instead of bringing a welcome coolness after the heat of the day, our upstairs apartment was still muggy and uncomfortable.

Harry didn't believe in air-conditioning, so we flung windows open in the hopes of catching any sea breeze. Ready for bed in my sleep tank and shorts, I was reminded of my duty to let Kit inside for the evening by the persistent scratching coming from the back door. His Lordship preferred not to use the cat door after an unfortunate tight-squeeze-almost-stuck incident.

I headed down the stairs in a zombie-like stagger and flung open the door, so Kit could zoom past me to investigate his food bowl. As I closed the door, a flash of white caught my eye. I yanked it open again.

Squinted.

Froze.

The white was a sheet of paper—copier paper, it looked like—and someone had pinned it to Nana Dee-Dee's potted lavender by a…?

Was that a…?

Yep, it was.

A knitting needle.

I didn't need to read the printed black letters on the paper. The knitting needle stabbed through the sheet was warning enough.

But I stumbled forward anyway and pulled the needle—a metal needle like the one my beginner class had used earlier—and paper from the plant's sweet-smelling foliage. The message was brief and to the point:

Keep your nose out of other people's business. Or else.

And below the words, a childish doodle of a cat, complete with whiskers and a curled tail. The point of the needle pierced the cat's chubby stomach.

ELEVEN

SLEEP TOOK its sweet time arriving that night.

After finding the note, I'd locked the cat door from the inside, so Pearl couldn't go out during the night as she often did. Then I completed a double and triple check of the downstairs doors and windows. Seemingly sensing my unease, both cats spent the night curled up on my bed. Kit stretched alongside my legs; Pearl tucked into a semi-circular punctuation mark near my pillow.

I woke early when the cats demanded they be let out. Wrapped in my fuzzy robe, I shoved the folded note into my pocket and made a steaming cup of coffee to take with me into the yard. I could keep an eye on the two mischief-makers and caffeinate at the same time.

While Kit and Pearl sniffed around Harry's glasshouse —the furry fiends could most likely smell the catnip growing inside—I checked the panels of my car. When I found no threats carved into the paintwork, I continued along the driveway to the gate.

Harry had hung a chain-link swing gate across the driveway soon after his 'unwanted' cats had arrived. It wasn't to keep them inside the property—never gonna happen with any feline—or as a security measure for him and Nana Dee-Dee. The gate was to keep dogs from hurting his 'little mates.' However, Pearl enjoyed teasing passing dogs with a feline version of a lap dance...just out of their reach behind the metal mesh.

Another fortifying sip of coffee under my belt, I made my way over to the gate latch. It wasn't latched. In fact, the gate was open. Only enough that a cat could squeeze through the gap, but open, nonetheless. The latch was tricky. If you weren't used to it, you'd think it had caught, but seconds later, the gate would start its slow creep open until it hit an uneven spot on the driveway and stuck.

I was one hundred percent sure I'd latched it yesterday evening.

Pearl weaved between my bare calves then parked her rear right on top of my slippers. My stomach wobbled as if I stood on the edge of a skyscraper. Who would threaten to hurt Kit and Pearl if I didn't stop asking questions? Logically, the person who killed Lucas. And, also logically, that meant the person must be a local.

I felt the damp press of a nose on my shin—a kitty kiss— and the soft vibration of Pearl's purr. Nana Dee-Dee loved these cats. Harry loves these cats. And even if I didn't love the little furballs myself, it infuriated me that some nameless, faceless coward would threaten to hurt an innocent creature. And, in doing so, break Harry's heart all over again.

There must be some way of figuring out who'd entered our yard last night. With one hand, I tugged the note from my pocket and awkwardly unfolded it, trying not to spill my coffee in the process. An errant gust caught the paper and whisked it over the gate, where it landed on the sidewalk, cat-doodle side up. I glanced wildly around for somewhere stable to set my coffee mug.

Priorities, right?

The paper skidded a few inches toward the gutter, and I dithered between the gate post, the ground—with the likelihood of the gate swinging open and knocking over the mug,

and just running with the coffee—thereby dooming myself to spill half of it down my robe. Have I mentioned I missed out on the evolutionary fight-or-flight response DNA? Not that I'd been put to the test, but I believed I was a ditherer, more of a possum frozen in a hunter's spotlight than a creature of action.

Pearl, however, didn't suffer from any such evolutionary setbacks. She leaped off my feet and streaked through the gap. Hunter after prey, she pounced. Except a running shoe got to the paper before her. A male-sized running shoe, belonging to a male-sized tanned and hairy leg, which in turn belonged to Oliver Novak, attired in running gear.

"This yours?"

My gaze reluctantly bid farewell to his athletically toned glutes and moved to his shoe, which precisely covered the writing and horrible cat doodle.

I nodded... I think.

My caffeine levels were still low enough that cognitive reasoning hadn't fully kicked in, but I was alert enough to mentally *uh-oh* when Oliver plucked the note from the ground. He glanced at it. I flinched when his eyes widened before tapering to hard slits as he finished reading.

He looked up, his mouth a grim slash.

"I found it skewered to a potted lavender by the back door last night. Someone's idea of a sick prank." I aimed for a nonchalant shrug but ended up with a shiver hard enough to slop coffee over the rim of my mug. Fortunately, it splattered on the ground, not on me.

"Skewered by what?" He lifted it to face height, examining the small hole.

"A knitting needle."

"An unusual choice. How did you find it?"

I gave him an abbreviated rundown of last night's knitting class, ending with my discovery of the note. "I didn't see or hear anything after everyone left the store, and it was nearly an hour later when I let Kit in. It was probably just bored kids looking for some summer entertainment. Freak out the old lady who plays with yarn and cats all day."

Oliver crossed the sidewalk to the gate and offered me the now crumpled note. I refolded it and shoved it back into the fuzzy depths of my robe pocket. He leaned against the gatepost, his greeny-blue eyes studying my *just rolled out of bed* face. Ugh. No mascara or anything. And worse... I clamped my lips shut, hoping I wasn't killing him with morning breath while resisting the temptation to cup my hand over my mouth to test it.

"You don't believe it was kids. And you're not old." A crinkle lifted the corner of his mouth. "The crazy is, as yet, undetermined."

What was almost a smile disappeared. "Someone left that note knowing it'd be you that found it this morning. They also know you care about these cats." He bent to scratch between Pearl's ears, and miraculously, she didn't shred his arm at the liberty he was taking. "Who do you think is panicked enough to threaten you?"

Exactly what I'd been asking myself. "Can't be Ed because he's had a night away from Discovery, courtesy of Napier Police."

"Agreed."

Pearl rolled onto her back, presenting her belly for Oliver's attention. Shameless hussy.

"An anonymous note doesn't strike me as Brian Werth's style," I said.

Considering I'd been completely vulnerable in his dentist's chair only a couple of days ago, I didn't want to contemplate what his style might be. 'Give 'im the old knuckle sandwich,' as Harry would say. And being a dentist, he could then add insult to injury by charging an exorbitant fee to repair the damage his meaty fist had caused.

"Agreed again." He used the tip of his running shoe to rub Pearl's belly. She purred. "Don't bite my head off for voicing a sexist stereotype, but a hand-drawn cartoon with the flourish of a knitting needle seems like something a woman would do."

"My turn to agree." I grimaced, remembering the look on Isabel's face last night when Beth had recited her little knitting rhyme. "And I think I know who it might be."

Oliver folded his arms and gave me the look I suspected he frequently used on customers trying to order another drink when they were obviously over the limit. "Leave it to the cops, Tessa. Don't be a hero."

Not bothering to hide my eye-roll, I said, "How about I just play it safe with my cats and yarn, all right?"

The mouth crinkle reappeared, and this time, it transformed into a grin that, okay, made me want to be a hero in his eyes. Fat chance of that, all things considered.

"You do that. I want you around to fulfill your debt to me in the near future." He pushed away from the gatepost and carefully stepped over Pearl's paint-me-like-one-of-your-French-girls pose. "Disco's ham and cheese croissant, remember? Heavy on the cheese." Then he picked up his feet into a run and loped off down the street.

I snickered at Pearl's haughty stare tracking Oliver's departure. In true cat fashion, she commenced grooming her hindquarters, as if the human's rejection of her advances was no skin off her tiny nose. My humor faded as I thought of the note. The idea of Isabel hurting Kit or Pearl didn't fit with the way she petted them in the store or fed them treats from her purse. Then again, murderers could love animals too, couldn't they?

And since I had almost two hours until Unraveled opened, there was plenty of time to pay the principal a visit.

IN A SIMILAR WAY that some men overcompensate for being short and bald by driving flashy sports cars, Isabel overcompensated for her cat allergy with her house decor theme: Everything Cat. From the cat-shaped mailbox to cat gnome ornaments lining the front path and her creepy door knocker—feline head with a mouse dangling from its mouth as a handle—Isabel missed the mark of kitschy-cute and landed in the center of *Hoarders: Crazy Cat Lady Edition*.

At just on eight, it was bright and sunny, with last night's rain showers already evaporating off the garden-proud yards I'd passed on my way to Isabel's. I knew where she lived thanks to Nana Dee-Dee's diligent note keeping. Often, when a customer ordered yarn she didn't have in stock, she'd personally delivered it on her 'daily constitutional' walk around the neighborhood when it arrived. Nana Dee-Dee had prided herself in providing customer service like no other, dropping off yarn and staying a while to chat if she thought that person could do with a spot of company and a smile.

Unraveled's delivery was due later this week—some of it yarn ordered by local regulars. Maybe I could take up Nana Dee-Dee's mantle of kindness toward elderly customers who found it difficult to get out.

Yeah. Except, did I really want to start something I didn't know I could continue?

Running a couple of classes was one thing; personal service, another. This was merely a time-out, temporary situation. If only I could get rid of the barrel roll of dread in my gut whenever I thought of leaving Harry, my family, and even the cats for greener pastures...

A worry for another day.

I marched past Isabel's cat gnome guards and, avoiding her rodent-chewing feline door knocker, used my knuckles instead. The knocking echoed hollowly inside, followed by silence. After what I deemed an appropriate length of time, I knocked again. Still nothing.

"She's not home, Miss," called a voice from next door.

I turned to see a man in a hot-pink bike helmet sitting astride a bicycle. With one hand balanced on a fence post and the other on the handlebars (prettily decorated with rainbow-colored streamers), he was giving me a head to toe. Perhaps wondering if I was about to indulge in some B&E.

"Has she gone out for the morning?"

The guy's face puckered into a frown. "Friend of hers, are you?"

Was I? Although I'd begun to like her in the short time that I'd known her, now I wasn't sure. But for all intents and purposes...

"Yes. I'm Tessa Wakefield—"

"Harry's granddaughter?" His bushy white eyebrows—a

stark contrast to his leathery, tanned skin—shot upward. "Why didn't you say so? I barely recognize you, girl. Your grandpa and me go way back. Dougie's my name. You tell him we miss him down the pub, and I'll shout him a beer next time he drops in."

"I will. Do you know where Isabel's gone?"

"Oh, aye. Not much happens down this end of the street, so a spot of drama sure gets the old ticker pumping."

"Drama?"

At my confused expression, Dougie chuckled. "Isabel slipped in her backyard last night, poor dear. What she was doing out there that late, I couldn't tell ya, but she sprained her ankle right good. Next door thataway"—he tipped his head toward the house on the other side of Isabel's—"drove her down to get it checked out at the hospital."

"And it's not broken?"

"Not even a fracture. Just a bad sprain, as I said. Got herself a moon boot and crutches, no less. She stayed at her sister's place in the city last night since they kept her waiting at the emergency department for hours. Sister's gonna drive her home later this morning, according to a text message Isabel sent me earlier. Along with a request for someone to water her tomato plants." He tutted. "Someone being me, of course, since she won't be pottering around in her garden anytime soon."

"Oh dear," I interrupted before Dougie could steamroll right over any attempt I might make to get more than one or two words out. "What time did she wake you up last night?" Kind of an odd question, but I hoped he wouldn't notice.

"I wasn't asleep." Dougie sounded insulted. "I'm not one of these old folks who're in bed by eight. I was watching telly when her car pulled in at about quarter past nine."

That sounded about right. She'd been one of the first wave of people to leave Unraveled last night.

He scratched a spot under his pink helmet in contemplation. "Saw her lights go on inside and not too long after, the outdoor ones went on as well. Nothing too unusual about that; the woman does love her tomatoes—and cats, as you might've noticed."

"I noticed."

"Then I wandered into the kitchen to make myself a cuppa, and I smelled smoke. Being a good neighbor, I checked out the window, but she was just burning something in the barbecue pit that her ex built shortly before he ran off with his tennis coach."

Judging by the gleam in Dougie's eye, he was dying to spill the details of *that* particular scandal.

"And that's when she sprained her ankle?" I asked.

"Sure was. Saw her do it too. Not that I routinely spy on my neighbors' nighttime adventures."

"Of course you don't," I murmured.

He tutted. "She tripped over one of the cherry tomato plants on the patio. Went down real hard and yelped like a kicked dog. I rushed over to help."

"She's lucky to have such a good neighbor." Inspiration struck. "Have you watered Isabel's tomatoes yet?"

"I was about to before I head into town."

"Why don't I save you the trouble? I'll pop out the back and give them a quick drink since I'm here and you're all ready to hit the road."

He beamed at me, the good Girl Scout. "Marvelous. I'll tell her you stopped by."

Uh-oh. I didn't want to give Isabel a heads-up that I'd been snooping. Hoping my innocent expression was firmly in place, I made a casual flicking away gesture. "No need.

I'll come back later to see if there's anything I can help with." I added my best Dionne Warwick smile. "That's what friends are for."

Dougie tipped me a salute and coasted down his driveway, streamers fluttering majestically as he pedaled away.

I retraced my steps from Isabel's front door and followed the path along the side of her house. More creepy lawn ornaments judged me as I tried to peer in the windows, though tightly closed drapes thwarted me at each one.

Around the back, I found a neatly mown lawn, inoffensive shrubs and flowerbeds, an old-fashioned rotary washing line, a wooden picnic table, and a patio area complete with brick barbecue as Dougie had described. I hurried over to the barbeque, my first stop, noting the upended broken planter on the patio. What Isabel had been doing out there became apparent when I spotted the mess of ash underneath the metal grill. She'd been torching something. From a couple of scraps, singed but not completely burned, I brilliantly deduced that *something* was photographs.

Quite a few of them, judging by the amount of ash.

After last night's class, I could make an educated guess as to who the star of the now destroyed photos was, but guesses weren't evidence.

From my vantage point on the raised patio, I rescanned Isabel's backyard in case I'd missed anything on first inspection. Nope. Just a nice suburban yard, in a nice suburban street, belonging to a nice suburban woman who liked gardening and cats and…

An object in a bushy pink rhododendron by the boundary fence caught my eye.

I crossed the lawn and plucked a singed but still intact photograph from the plant's leaves. The photo was a selfie of Isabel and Lucas on Cape Discovery Beach. Lucas stared directly into the camera lens, flashing a toothpaste-commercial smile. Tucked under his arm, Isabel clung to him, gazing up at his face with an expression that could only be described as adoring.

Desperately adoring.

Head over heels in lust, or maybe even love, adoring.

Isabel had flat-out lied about her relationship with Lucas, and by the sound of things, it hadn't been a match made in heaven. Hell hath no fury, indeed. But it was also unlikely Isabel had left the threatening note at my door last night. Unlikely, but not impossible.

After staring at the photo a moment longer, I tucked it into the front pocket of my shirt, very much aware of the folded note and the leprechaun pin in my shorts pocket. A veritable smorgasbord of hidden secrets: that was me.

Hearing a scuff behind me, I jerked around in an ungainly hop. And came face to face with an arms-folded, suit-molded-to-muscles-wearing, thoroughly ticked-off-looking detective.

TWELVE

THE ONE THING Detective Mana didn't look was surprised to see me. I decided to brazen it out.

"Good morning, Eric," I called out, adding a cheery little wave in case he'd missed the perkiness of my tone.

He didn't wave back. His block-like arms remained folded, his gaze unreadable behind his wraparound sunglasses. But I didn't need to see his dried-concrete-colored eyes to know they weren't crinkled with good humor.

"Why are you here?" His voice was grit and crushed gravel.

"Being neighborly and watering Isabel's tomatoes. See?" I picked up a nearby watering can, which, thank goodness, made a sloshing sound when I lifted it. I proceeded to demonstrate my competent irrigation technique. "Why are *you* here? Top secret official police business?"

His only response was a muscle flexing on one side of his carved-from-granite jaw.

I held the watering can above another tomato plant. Not having inherited a green thumb from either Harry or my dad, I hoped I didn't drown the poor thing. "Isabel isn't home at the moment."

He cocked his head. "*Really?* Do you know where she is?"

Opting to play nice, I smiled a *helpful citizen* smile. "Yes, Detective. She's on her way back from her sister's place in Napier."

The detective's eyebrows arrowed down. "Does she know you're trespassing on her property?"

Okay, forget about nice then. The best defense is a good offense—a polite offense, anyway. After all, I didn't want to get arrested. "Isabel's a long-standing member of my grandmother's knitting group. And also, ah, my friend."

Which didn't clarify whether I had her express permission to be there. But then something occurred to me, and thanks to a sometimes filter malfunction in my brain, I blurted it out: "What are *you* doing in her backyard? Don't you need a warrant or something?"

Eric pushed his shades onto his head and strode over to the patio. His long legs ate up the distance so rapidly that I didn't have time to brace myself for the full impact of his way-too-close presence. He stopped less than a foot from me and grabbed hold of my wrist.

As I let out a shocked yelp, the watering can dropped from my hand, and water splattered the bottom of his suit pants.

He released my wrist so quickly I thought I'd imagined the warmth of his fingers on my skin. "Sorry, I didn't mean to startle you. You were drowning the tomato."

Sucked that he was right. A pool of water spread out from the base of the planter. Drowning by misadventure, or perhaps drowning by the distraction of a woman susceptible to a man in a well-tailored suit. Whichever.

"And to answer your question," he continued, moving his expensive-looking leather shoes away from the puddle, "I knew you were back here somewhere and wanted to know why."

My facial features must have rearranged themselves into a caricature of skepticism because faint lines of amusement feathered from the corners of his lips. "I'm not psychic; if that's what you're thinking."

He looked over his shoulder, in the direction of the driveway.

I followed his gaze to Isabel's buttercup yellow car, and the black cat grooming its hindquarters on top of it.

Pearl.

"Is that her name?" Eric said.

I hadn't realized I'd spoken out loud. Slanting a glance at him, I noted the faint lines around his mouth had expanded into what could almost be mistaken for a smile.

"She's very diligent in her grooming," I said.

Ignoring us, Pearl continued to give one hundred percent of her attention to her nether regions.

"Cleanliness is next to godliness," I muttered.

"Cats think they *are* gods, don't they?"

When I stared at him—somewhat in disbelief that this big, grim-looking detective actually had a sense of humor—he gestured over his shoulder. "There's another one sitting under the mailbox out front. That's the one I saw first. I assume it's the other cat mentioned in the official statement you made last week?"

"Yes. That'd be Kit. He and Pearl are siblings. They go everywhere together."

Why I felt compelled to explain their relationship to a man—not just any man, but a high-ranking police officer who had the authority to cuff me and frog-march me to his police car—I had no idea.

My only dealings with the police—other than Harry, of course—had been a speeding ticket and chatting with some user-friendly officers at a high school careers event. Neither interaction had left me tongue-tied one moment, babbling the next, or feeling like I'd eaten undercooked chicken and was playing food-poisoning Russian Roulette. Would I or wouldn't I start throwing up in the next ten minutes...

"Everywhere together, while following you? Like a close protection team?"

"Yeah. Something like that." Add inexplicably defensive to the tongue-tied or babbling. "The cats were my grandmother's, and since she passed away last year, they've kept me under surveillance."

"They're afraid you'll disappear out of their world too, and then there'll be no one to watch them back." Something dark and a little bit lonely flickered in his eyes. He returned the shades to his face and shoved his fists into the pockets of his suit pants. "Tell me why you're really here, Tessa."

Both the photograph and the threatening note felt like acid, burning holes in my pockets. I wasn't ready to admit the surveillance I was under was not of the cute feline kind. What I wanted was for the investigation to direct its piercing gaze on a suspect other than my brother. I dragged out the photograph of Lucas and Isabel and offered it to him.

Eric examined the photo, holding it carefully by one singed corner, blank expression firmly in place. His head shifted for a moment as he scanned the barbecue area, then the insect-like gaze of his reflective shades swept back to me. "You found this where?"

Fifty Shades of Cop had returned to his tone, making

my stomach give a nervous hiccup. "Caught in the rhododendron. It must've blown out of the fire when she burned the others."

"Did you see Ms. Burton burning these items?"

I shook my head. "Her neighbor told me. He was watching when she tripped and hurt herself."

At the twitch of his eyebrow, I caved and repeated everything Dougie had told me. After listening without interrupting until I ran out of steam, he withdrew a plastic bag from his jacket pocket and slipped the photo inside.

Eric sidestepped around me and crossed the patio to take a closer look at the remains of Isabel's late-night cookup. Like a helpless insect drawn to his charismatic light, I trailed after him. We stood, side by side, peering down at the ashy remains.

"What do you make of this ritualistic burning of photographs?"

I gave him a startled side-eyed blink. The detective sergeant was asking for my opinion? Heat crept up my throat, warming my vocal cords and, weirdly, making me want to purr like a stroked kitten.

"Oh." I focused on the evenly stacked bricks while gathering my flailing thoughts. "I think Isabel had very strong feelings for Lucas. Feelings that weren't reciprocated in the way she wanted."

"Strong enough feelings for her to kill him if he rejected her?"

"I don't know," I said with complete honesty. "Everyone has to learn how to handle rejection, and we all deal with it in our own way. Some more violently than others, granted. You must see that a lot in your line of work."

He gave a soft grunt that sounded like affirmation. "Far too much, and far too often." He used a finger to push his shades onto his head again. Eric now; RoboCop Detective had been relegated to riding shotgun. "Let's say, for argument's sake, you were involved with a man who you thought was as into you as you were into him. Would you key his home and burn photos of him if he broke off this little dalliance?"

The side-eye I gave him this time wasn't startled but grudgingly impressed. Detective Mana knew more than I'd suspected. "Dalliance? What are you, eighty?"

He almost cracked a smile. Almost.

"Ed told you about Isabel and the RV, huh?"

"With enthusiasm."

"Score one for you."

He made a sound that could have been a chuckle. "Back to my hypothetical question, which I'll preface by saying, I acknowledge that all women are unique individuals—"

"Yeah, yeah." Thanks to Jared, I was intimately acquainted with rejection and its sidekick, humiliation. "Would I burn his photos?"

I'd packed up photos of my ex and put them in storage, along with years of accumulated stuff that I had no idea what to do with. Would I burn them, though? No. It was enough that those photos would sit in dusty cardboard boxes until, one day, they'd be faded memories, sorted through along with ticket stubs and old letters and thrown into a recycling bin. I refused to give him free rental space in my brain, even if it was just to fill it with the ashes of photographs taken in happier times.

But—as far as I knew—Isabel hadn't been in a long-term relationship with Lucas Kerr. From the outside, it appeared to have been a summer fling. In which case...

"Burn, shred, draw devil's horns on. Yep, more than likely. But keying a guy's RV? That's a whole 'nother level.

My granddad's a retired cop; rules and staying on the right side of the law is in my genetics."

"Really?"

"Really, really. Although, as a pirate once said: 'Rules are more like guidelines.' Sometimes I bend them a bit."

This time I got a proper smile. And, wow, Detective Sergeant Eric Mana actually looked human when he smiled. I found myself smiling back until I remembered the point he was trying to make with his hypothetical question. Was a woman in lust/love capable of murdering a man who, for some reason, made her want to vandalize his property in anger? On that, I couldn't speak from personal experience.

"You're speculating on whether a woman could be driven to lash out in a fit of passion. But I can't give you a solid answer because I've never felt that intensity of emotion for another person."

"Never been in love?"

This definitely wasn't an officer of the law asking, and my pulse fluttered like a panicked bird. I didn't want to get introspective with this man. He unsettled me in ways I didn't care to examine. "Of course I have. Just not to the extent that I'd pay a guy a visit in the middle of the night, drug him, then bash him over the head with a wine bottle."

As soon as the words pattered out of my mouth, I longed to suck them back in. One blessed moment of wishful thinking that Eric hadn't picked up on my slip, and then—

"How do you know Lucas was drugged? That information wasn't released to the public."

I tucked my lips together and imagined staples holding them shut.

He sighed, pinching the spot between his eyebrows as if he had a headache developing. A headache named Tessa

Wakefield. "I can make an educated guess as to what little birdie gave you that information."

"Let's just say it's hard to keep secrets in Cape Discovery." And yet, quite a few of its residents seemed to. "Please don't blame my granddad. He was only trying to help."

"Like you're trying to help clear your brother's name?"

"I am." I turned to face him and adopted what I hoped was my sincerest *honesty is my middle name* expression. "He didn't do this, Eric. You must know that now."

Using his first name might be pushing the limits of our acquaintance too far, but he didn't seem to mind.

He sighed again. "Unofficially, Sean is no longer our prime suspect. We received an anonymous tip-off"—his eyes narrowed into suspicious slits—"*another* anonymous tip-off, that a woman fitting Isabel's description was seen at the pop-up store late on the night Lucas was murdered."

So that's why the detective was paying Isabel a visit. "Was the caller male or female?"

"They disguised their voice, but we think it was a man."

My brain spun with possibilities. "A man? But what if...?"

Eric stepped away from me with a grimace. "No more 'what-ifs.' You need to walk away now and let me do my job. We can take it from here."

Lucas Kerr's murderer was still on the loose, and pardon me for noticing, the police seemed no closer to catching her. Or him...

Although Eric-the-detective had tolerated my interference so far, I wasn't deluded enough to believe I could continue debating with him.

I showed him both palms. "Backing off, Detective. As of this moment, I will only use my crime-solving skills to find out who broke into the pantry and chewed off the end of a fresh loaf of bread."

"Good luck with that." The look that followed was clearly meant to dissuade me from any further chitchat.

Let the professionals be professional. Right.

With a cheery wave instead of a rebellious middle finger —not that I would, but I could be a rebel, if only in my head —I stalked away from Isabel's house.

The anonymous tip-off Eric mentioned kept niggling at the back of my mind. If the caller was telling the truth, Isabel had lied about never visiting the store after hours. And who'd been out at that time of night, in that particular part of town, close enough to recognize Isabel?

Because whoever made that call could be an innocent witness...or they could be the killer.

BY LUNCHTIME THE NEXT DAY, I needed to get some fresh air before I truly did turn into a crazy cat lady. Or a cantankerous one, more accurately.

Everything had got up my proverbial nose since my encounter with the tall, dark, and irritatingly smug detective yesterday. Unraveled's customers were more demanding than usual. Kit was constantly under my feet, trying to herd me in the direction of his food bowl. Pearl left a disemboweled mouse on my pillow. My mum had insisted I come to dinner tonight—and I could only get out of it if a bus ran me over and I was in a medically induced coma. Even Harry wasn't his usual cheerful self.

Not to mention my own frustration at being back at ground zero, trying to figure out who'd murdered Lucas Kerr.

An hour tops, I told myself as I flipped over the 'Back in a Tick!' sign and slipped out Unraveled's front door. One hour without customers, cats, or thinking about killers. I'd stroll along the beach and then afterward pick up some delicious treats for the Crafting for Calmness class tonight. Hard to believe it was nearly a week since I'd stumbled upon Lucas's body...

And there went my vow not to think about killers.

The main street seemed busier than usual. As my gaze swept over both strangers and locals, I didn't know who I was looking for until I spotted Dylan Werth entering the Daily Grind. If I had to start from scratch, go back to the drawing board, hit reset, and every other cliché that meant I'd struck out on the amateur sleuthing front, then talking to Dylan again was as good a place as any to start. He still hadn't given me a satisfactory explanation as to why he'd been hanging around Lucas Kerr. Perhaps I could find out more without his parents lurking in the background.

A visit to Rosie's café twice in one week wasn't as unpleasant as line dancing in your underwear, but it was close. Sure enough, Rosie herself stood at the cash register, most likely rubbing her hands together in glee at the influx of customers wanting scoops of her overpriced homemade gelato since the day was so warm.

Dylan had joined the line, which was long enough that he stood only a step inside the door. To pass the time while he waited, he stared at the community noticeboard—filled with printed flyers about roommates wanted, lost animals, garage sales, and the like.

I sidled up behind him and peered around him, trying to see what had captured his attention. Ah, the fundraising photo competition.

Win $200 in vouchers! Which of these Cape Discovery

locals do you recognize? Gold coin donation to enter. All proceeds go to Cape Discovery's after-school Kidz Club.

Below the headline was a dozen color photocopied photos of kids, ranging from drooling babies to chubby-faced preschoolers. I hadn't had time to enter the competition, but I immediately recognized my mum's frizzy hair and Harvey, the scruffy white rabbit she was cuddling and still owned. A few of the other kids had features that remained into adulthood. No one could miss hair salon owner Angelica Wigham's piercing green eyes.

As Dylan became aware of me hovering behind his arm, I swear he flinched. "Oh. Hey," he said amicably enough, but his gaze flicked back to the photos. "Isn't number three your mum?"

"Have you entered yet?" I matched his *just being friendly* tone. "Because confirming that number three is my mum would give you an unfair advantage."

He gave a small chuckle. "Nah. The vouchers are all for dumb stuff like manicures and ten free coffees. I don't drink coffee."

Funny, because right now, Dylan was jittering like a deprived caffeine addict.

He shrugged his skinny shoulders. "Besides, I already have an unfair advantage; Brian's on the Kidz Club board of trustees, and I helped him scan all the photos and format the sign because, you know, technology and the olds don't mix."

I gave him my most reassuring harmless-grown-up smile. "I bet he sends you text messages all in capitals too."

Dylan rolled his eyes. Then he pointed to a couple of photos and told me who they were. "Most of the others are pretty obvious."

He tapped another photo, this one featuring two young

girls in matching party dresses, blowing out candles on a bright-green frosted birthday cake. "That's my mum and her sister."

The two girls bore a striking resemblance to each other. "Twins?"

"Yep."

The line began to move, and we inched past the noticeboard. I wanted to keep Dylan talking. "You hanging out with friends today?" I asked.

His shoulders sagged, and he shoved his hands into the pockets of his baggy shorts. "Maybe this afternoon. Got some chores and study to do first."

"Not your idea, I take it."

A shrug. "Brian's."

"Ah." I dipped my chin toward the shelves of healthy-looking sandwiches and filled rolls. "You're making a supply run, huh?"

His gaze flicked longingly over to where an assistant scooped gelato into waffle cones. "Yep. Been let out for an hour on good behavior."

Not above a touch of bribery, I pointed toward the freezer. "How about I spring for an ice cream that you can eat before you're incarcerated again?"

"You're offering to buy me ice cream?" His voice was filled with an unspoken *what's the catch?*

"If we can have a chat outside?"

Dylan screwed up his nose as he considered my offer. Then he shrugged, as I'd hoped he would. Free junk food in exchange for letting some weird lady talk his ear off for ten minutes...? Sounded fair.

"Double scoop."

The kid was playing hardball. "Deal."

Rosie didn't say anything snarky when she asked what I

wanted, but her sharp gaze darted from me to Dylan when I ordered two gelatos.

"I wanted to thank you for the extra goodies you gave me last week," I added while she keyed in our order.

"You're welcome," she said without looking at me.

While Dylan wandered off to decide what flavors he wanted, I endured Rosie's silent judgment for as long as I could. Approximately ten seconds.

"It's not what you think." I dug around in my shoulder bag for my wallet.

"You've no idea what I'm thinking." Rosie drummed inch-long nails on the service counter.

Little Ms. Impatience. *I'd show her*. I plucked the wallet triumphantly from my bag and proceeded to count out the exact change in a few months' accumulation of loose coins.

"Do I want to?" I took in her raised—and perfectly groomed—eyebrows and shook my head. "On second thoughts, don't answer that." I plonked three one dollar coins and two fifty cent coins on the counter. Rummaged some more. "Your opinion of me couldn't drop much lower."

"Don't underestimate yourself." Rosie's grin reminded me of a small, cute mammal with a mouthful of razor-sharp teeth. She folded her arms on the service counter and leaned in. "You still trying to find out who killed Lucas Kerr?"

I froze mid-transfer of a handful of twenty and ten cent coins, which I'd intended to make Rosie count. Yeah, petty. But if I'd failed to beat her at her mind games through high school, I could grub some small satisfaction from hoping she'd break a nail counting coins.

I was drawn down into a co-conspirator's pose. "Do you know something?"

Her gaze slid left, to where Dylan tapped the glass above one of the flavors.

"You'll know this about teenagers already," she murmured, "but when a bunch of them get together, some sort of herd mentality occurs. They feel safe in their circle of friends and can get caught up in being the cool kid in the group—the ram amongst the sheep, so to speak—and forget there are predators nearby."

I blinked at her. "Huh? Teenagers are cool-kid sheep, and you're suggesting I'm a predator?"

She rolled her eyes as, with one hot-pink painted fingernail, she tapped my fist, which was still clenched around the damp, sweaty coins. I released them, and they plinked onto the counter, a few rolling off onto the hardwood floor. As we both crouched to retrieve them, I came face to face with Rosie under the counter gap.

With a soft hiss of frustration, she tried to pry up a stubborn ten cent coin and glared at me. "Listen. Late last year, I heard Dylan and his school buddies talking about extra study aids."

"Those caffeine-heavy energy drinks?"

"That's what I thought at first. Kerr's name cropped up, but I still didn't put two and two together until the cops discovered what was in Lucas's storeroom."

"Oh, no—you mean *drug* study aids?"

Rosie gave me another eyebrow raise that said, *Well, duh.* And I'd earned it. The years I'd spent working with teenagers who struggled with many different issues, including incredible pressure during exam time, should have raised a giant red flag that something more sinister than stress could be involved. But I'd become complacent, assuming the most dangerous problem teenagers encountered in Cape Discovery was a riptide at one end of the beach.

"I had no idea." But it went a long way toward explaining Isabel's comments about Dylan being 'off' during his exams last year. "I was about to ask him again why he was hanging around Lucas's store."

Rosie straightened and dumped the coins back onto the counter. Counting, she scraped them one by one into her palm. I didn't dare interrupt her tally; instead, I picked up a bunch of paper napkins.

"Here." She slid a couple of coins back to me. "Whatever Dylan had to do with Lucas, he's a good kid. Tutored my eldest boy in math a few times when he fell behind."

"I'll keep that in mind. Lovely to see you again, Rosie."

That earned me another eye-roll. Probably deserved that one too.

Stowing my almost weightless wallet back in my bag, I strolled over and directed Rosie's assistant to construct me a cone of raspberry gelato.

Ice creams in hand, Dylan and I walked out of the Daily Grind and crossed the road to the seawall, where we sat and dangled our feet. Once I'd gained lick-control of my rapidly melting gelato, I turned toward Dylan with my sternest former-guidance-counselor stare. The one that had netted me all sorts of confessions in the past.

"Tell me about the study aids you bought off Lucas Kerr."

THIRTEEN

A FAINT RING of chocolate around his mouth, Dylan gaped at me, looking more like a terrified preschooler than a young man rapidly approaching legal adulthood.

"Uhh." His gaze skittered away to the beach, perhaps in a silent plea for help from a waddling seagull eyeing up his ice cream.

"Just to warn you, I've heard every possible excuse invented by teenage minds, and I'll know if you're lying."

I continued to lick my cone, slowly, luxuriating in the silky sweetness. As if I had all the time in the world to listen to his confession. Had to give Rosie her dues: The gelato was delicious.

"How come? Are you a doctor or something?"

"Guidance counselor at a high school in Auckland." *Former* guidance counselor. But he didn't need to know that. "You'll get no judgment from me, but I want to know the truth." Hopefully, he was naïve enough not to realize he didn't have to tell me diddly-squat, let alone the truth.

Dylan resumed eating his cone while giving me the side-eye. After a few licks, he paused. "But you are kind of like a doctor or shrink or something? You can't, like, tell my parents, because of patient confidentiality, right?"

Eh, not so much. As per my previous thought, *former* counselor. But again, this was on a need-to-know basis, and Dylan didn't need to know. "Sure."

He stared challengingly at me for another beat before his shoulders sagged. "I only bought the pills to help me get through exams; I wasn't trying to get wasted."

"What sort of pills?" I asked.

A shrug. The kind unique to the under-twenty-five crowd, who thought youth made them invincible, no matter what they subjected their bodies to. "Lucas said they'd give me loads of energy and help me focus on nailing the exams."

"How did you find out Lucas was selling pills?"

"Some mates." He shook his head. "I won't nark on them if that's what you're asking."

"No. I understand how word gets around school. Exam time's pretty stressful, especially when last year's results can determine which university you'll get into."

"Yeah," he said gloomily. "I just hope I've done better than scrape through; otherwise I might end up like Lucas." He bit into the wafer cone with a crunch and scrambled to his feet. "Thanks for the ice cream, but I gotta go."

Shading my eyes from the blinding midday sun, I squinted up at him. "You're welcome. But, hey, do you think your parents know you took pills?"

Dylan barked out a short laugh. "No way. They would've killed me if they found out." His brow furrowed. "You won't say anything to them, will you?"

Not if I didn't have to. "Planning to do drugs again, Dylan?"

He swiped the back of his hand across his chocolate-smeared mouth. "Nah. The crash after the buzz wasn't worth it. So, we good?"

"We're good."

He jogged away, the seagull who'd been spying on him now circling above his head, waiting for the kid to drop a tidbit. I brushed crumbs off my legs and stood. Closing my eyes, I let the sound of the waves hissing ashore, the fresh scent of salt and seaweed, and the warmth of the sunshine on my upturned face steady me.

Aside from my determination to discover who'd killed Lucas—I was invested now, and I blamed my stubborn mule-headedness on the Wakefield side of the family—I had the more personal issue of figuring out what to do next in my life. Summer was half over, and I couldn't continue freeloading off Harry while I made up my mind.

I sighed, knowing I'd hear all about it and much more over tonight's family dinner.

But as I made my way back to Unraveled—more locals recognized me now and stopped me to chat—one thought kept bouncing around in my brain. Dylan had jokingly said his parents would kill him if they found out he'd experimented with drugs. But what if they *had* found out?

Would they have murdered the man who'd sold them to their son?

BEING SUMMONED to a family dinner by my mother meant one of two things: a sibling had done something right and was worth boasting about, or I'd done something wrong. That was possibly an unfair generalization, but it felt true in the same way that the oldest sibling is often the bossiest and the youngest is often the most spoiled.

Usually, Dad opened the front door while my mother barked out orders like an army general to whichever of my siblings she'd cornered in the kitchen. Tonight, however, instead of Dad's sheepish but warm smile greeting me, Mum threw open the door. Before I could ask why she was smiling *at me*, she wrapped me in a boa constrictor hug. "Thank you, thank you, thank you."

My face scrunched up above the chin I'd rested on her shoulder. What on earth was she thanking me for? Surely not the bottle of grocery store wine I held in one hand? "Um, sure, Mum. No worries."

I drew back and thrust the wine at her. "It's just a cheap chardonnay, but I know you like this one."

She took the bottle from my hand and looked at me as if I'd developed a sudden concussion on the walk to the family home. "I'm not thanking you for the wine, silly girl. I'm thanking you for what you've been doing for your brother; for restoring his good reputation around town."

I wouldn't go so far as to say Sean had a good reputation before Lucas Kerr inconveniently got himself killed. But when it came to Mum, I'd take whatever praise I could get.

"He's family. Of course I'd do anything for him."

Patting my arm, she peered around me. "Where's Harry?"

"Getting ready for the Crafting for Calmness class this evening. He's baking a cake, though I saw him dump grated carrot in the mixing bowl, so I think he's forgotten he's making a banana cake." I chuckled, remembering his barely contained excitement as the afternoon wore on—like a kid waiting for his birthday party guests to arrive. "Don't worry, I made him soup and a sandwich for dinner."

Appearing mollified, she waved me inside. "Of course

you did. Dad and I are so grateful and proud of the good care you take of Harry."

Now I truly felt as though I'd stepped into some sort of weird alternative universe, one where it was possible my mum approved of, or at least accepted my life choices.

"He'll miss you when you get your life back on track and find a *real* job," she added as I followed her into the dining room.

Aaaaand back to reality with a crash.

Sean was already seated at the table, and on overhearing Mum's last comment, he rolled his eyes at me in solidarity. I took my place next to him while Dad set down the serving platter of roast lamb with a flourish.

Dinner passed in a blur of mint sauce, crispy roasted potatoes, and *Tales from a Real Estate Agent*, with Mum doing most of the talking. As usual. However, I was grateful for hers and Sean's constant chatter because it meant I got to eat without interruption. Plus, I could replay my conversations with Dylan and his parents over and over, searching for new clues.

I still hadn't come up with any startling revelations when Mum mentioned something about Dad having a toothache and being typically stubborn about getting it checked out.

"Speaking of the dentist," I said, interrupting Mum's pestering offer to book him an appointment, "did you know Jennifer Werth has a twin sister?"

My parents stopped mid-bicker, and Mum stared at me with an exasperated expression. "This isn't exactly an earth-shattering revelation, sweetie. I sold a house to Mrs. Foster, who used to be the family's neighbor. Jennifer doesn't talk about her sister, though. Julia, I think her name was."

"Black sheep of the family, eh? That why doesn't she talk about her?" Dad asked the question before I could.

Dad was a second-generation Cape Discovery local, but unlike my mum, he didn't feel the need to know everything about everybody.

'This doesn't concern you, so mind your own beeswax,' was one of his favorite pieces of advice. That and, 'Not my circus, not my monkeys,' whenever Mum grilled him for any town gossip he'd heard while on his deliveries.

Mum's mouth puckered into a grimace. "When I sold the house, I told you about Jennifer and her twin. Weren't you listening?"

Dad winked at me. "Course I was. Just refresh my memory." He completely tuned out when Mum got going on one of her gossip sagas.

After a long-suffering sigh, Mum spoke. "It's not really dinner table conversation, but"—she leaned forward in a dramatic pause—"according to Mrs. Foster, Jennifer and Julia were like chalk and cheese. Jennifer was the girl who studied hard and got good grades, whereas her sister struggled to keep up. Mrs. Foster thought maybe she had a touch of dyslexia. Regardless, things went bad for the twins when they moved to Auckland, so Jennifer could attend university. While her twin studied, Julia decided to have a gap year and got herself a job in retail. She also decided she liked being eighteen and old enough to paint the town red, with or without her sister. Mrs. Foster said the girls' parents didn't seem too concerned about reports of wild behavior from the family member they were boarding with. That was until one Friday night when Julia went into the city alone with friends."

Mum closed her eyes for a moment, and in her face, I saw sadness and empathy, not merely someone repeating a juicy nugget of gossip. "She didn't come home that night. The next morning, police arrived to inform the girls' parents that Julia's body had been found at the base of a multistory parking garage. She'd either fallen or jumped, and a pair of eyewitnesses who'd seen her earlier claimed she'd been as high as a kite."

"How awful," I said. "That poor family."

With a nod, Mum folded her napkin into a neat square and set it on top of her plate. "I think Jennifer took it the hardest. Not only had she lost her twin, and in such horrible circumstances, but she also blamed herself for not being with her sister that night to stop her from doing something stupid."

No wonder Jennifer didn't talk about her.

"That sucks." Sean rocked his chair back onto two legs. "But how about we talk about something less depressing, like, is there any dessert?"

"Not for me," I said, and using Harry and the upcoming class as an excuse, I made my escape.

TEN MINUTES LATER, I let myself in through the back door of Unraveled and came face-to-face with Kit and Pearl, who eyeballed me with accusing stares. From above came loud TV voices, and I grinned when I recognized the host's voice from *MasterChef*. Harry was definitely getting himself in the mood for the meeting. Also drifting down the stairs was the delicious smell of cake.

Time check—I still had an hour before the group was due to arrive. I'd promised Harry I'd be back for the start of the meeting and, having organized everything other than the cake he'd baked, I could still duck out for one last errand without causing him to fret.

As I scratched Kit under his chin, and he chirped with pleasure, Pearl stretched and sauntered over to sit beside her empty food dish. Her *downstairs* food dish. That's right, they had bowls upstairs and downstairs. Spoiled, much?

"Subtle kitty, aren't you?" I whispered. "But I've already fed you, and you'll get treats from Isabel later... Oh, wait, no you won't. Sorry."

I hadn't spoken to Isabel in person, though I'd left a 'hope you feel better soon' message on her voicemail. But I doubted we'd see her at tonight's class. Thinking of Isabel led me to tussle again with the suspicion she was Lucas's killer, even though a few things didn't add up.

Like the note threatening Kit and Pearl: cats she clearly doted on. Not to mention the timing of it being left in my yard. And the leprechaun pin. It didn't strike me as Isabel's style, not when the woman had a yard full of cat-themed knickknacks.

And then there was the revelation about Jennifer Werth's twin sister, who'd died tragically when they were teenagers...in what sounded like a drug-related incident.

Coincidence?

That was the purpose of my quick errand. If given fifteen minutes alone with the woman and a cup of tea, I was confident my counseling background could be used to coax out more detail. Finding Jennifer's home address was easy. And with a quick snatch-and-grab of a few balls of yarn from Unraveled shelves and some cellophane and ribbon, I'd created the perfect excuse to drop in on her unannounced.

Brian and Jennifer lived on one of the prettiest roads in Cape Discovery. It was lined with native pohutukawa trees, a few still retaining their crimson quill-like blossoms despite being known as New Zealand's Christmas tree because of the vibrant blooms that peaked in late December every year. Set back from the road, the Werths' two-story house was surrounded by a neatly trimmed privacy hedge and had a circular driveway that wouldn't have looked out of place at a four-star boutique hotel's entrance. There were no cars in the driveway, but with an attached three-door garage, they might have been parked up for the night.

I pressed the doorbell and listened to its chime echo inside, clutching the packaged yarn in front of me like a shield. A blurred Orc-sized shadow appeared behind the frosted glass door and morphed into the grim-faced dentist when he flung it open.

However, his grim expression evaporated as he locked eyes with me, replaced by a smile that didn't reach his eyes. "Hello. Tessa, isn't it?" he said. "What brings you here? Hopefully, not an after-hours dental emergency, heh-heh."

Holding up the yarn, I returned his smile, hoping it appeared friendly. "We had a door prize at the beginners knitting class Jennifer attended last week, and she won!" Had I sounded too bright, too excitably enthusiastic? Maybe a tad hysterical? I cleared my throat and aimed to lower my voice at least half an octave. "Is your wife around?"

I tried to peer past his bulk into the house's interior, but he partially closed the door. "Sorry, she's got a bit of a headache, so she's resting."

"Oh."

He extended a hand through the now narrow gap between door and doorframe. "I can give this to her later when she wakes up."

But I kept my fingers wrapped tightly around the package. "I'd really like to speak to her. I wanted to apologize for all the talk about drugs and drug dealing during the class."

Brian stared at me, muscles bunching in his jaw as if he were grinding his molars together. That couldn't be good for his teeth.

Spurred by an adrenaline rush as I imagined him with a dentist's drill in his hand, my tongue continued to waggle. "Honestly, I had no idea about her sister, and I feel terrible that our discussion might've brought up some painful memories. To lose a sibling that way and then the shocking discovery of a drug dealer in town; I thought she might like to talk..."

As I paused to whoop in more oxygen, instead of shutting the door in my face, he opened it wide. "Come in, then. I'll go see if Jennifer's awake."

The foyer of the Werths' house was every bit as impressive as the paved entranceway. However, I didn't have long to admire the curved staircase leading upstairs, as Brian ushered me into the living room. Two huge leather couches and a massive wall-mounted television dominated the room, a space large enough to hold half of her grandparents' apartment.

Perched on the edge of a couch, I tipped my head, trying to hear what was going on upstairs. Brian's deep voice was a distant rumble, and after a minute, the sound of running water drifted down the stairs. Heavy footfalls followed, and I glanced around to see him with his *open wide; this won't hurt a bit* professional face affixed firmly in place.

"Sorry about that," he said smoothly before lowering his voice in a faux confidential manner. "Jen gets a bit cranky if she's woken up. But she's happy to talk to you; she's just hopping in the shower first."

"Okay," I said. "I'm a bit cranky too if my nap's interrupted."

He angled himself back toward the doorway. "I'd better follow orders and make you both a hot drink. Tea okay?"

"Fine, thanks. Milk and two sugars please."

Brian bustled away, and through the doorway came the clink of china and the rumble of an electric kettle heating. I leaned back into the cushions—surprisingly plush and comfortable, they gave me a moment of couch envy—and attempted to organize my galloping thoughts. It was much like herding kittens.

One errant thought kept jumping above the crowd and waving its arms in a frantic bid for attention: What if Dylan's comment about his exam results and 'ending up like Lucas' didn't mean what I'd assumed it meant. That he'd be 'dead' if he didn't do well in his exams.

What if he'd meant if he didn't do well, he might end up like Lucas, selling drugs to schoolkids?

And how would the Werths feel about their kid becoming a drug dealer? Especially Brian, who obviously had some big ambitions for his stepson. But before I could fling myself headlong down that side street of inquiry, Brian reappeared with two cups and saucers.

"There we go," he said, handing one to me. After setting the other down on the smoked-glass coffee table, he lowered himself onto the couch opposite me and crossed his legs.

The fabric of his trousers made a whispery sound, inexplicably sending a shudder of distaste rippling over my scalp. I sipped at the tea, which was strong and sweet, just the way I liked it. Although I couldn't imagine ever being relaxed in this man's presence—he'd scraped tartar off my teeth, so, eww—he did make a decent cuppa.

"So, what's with this sleuthing hobby Jen tells me

you've taken up recently?" Brian draped his arms over the back of the couch. "Were you close to the deceased, or are you just trying to get one up on that arrogant city detective?"

Forget his brewing skills, the man was as tactful as a septic tank truck spewing its sloppy cargo into a swimming pool. "Detective Mana is just doing his job."

"If he were doing his job, he would've arrested Isabel Burton by now."

"Do you really think she did it?" I swallowed more tea. If I were completely honest, it could've done with being hotter, but at least it was drinkable. My mouth felt weirdly dry, so I took another gulp.

He lifted a shoulder. "Crime of passion, I reckon. Wouldn't surprise me if she was in on the drug dealing too. What better setup than working with all those teenagers who want to experiment?"

Wow, a huge jump in logic from crime of passion to partners in crime. However, I was more interested in his relationship with Lucas Kerr than Isabel's. He had physically threatened Lucas for flirting with his wife.

But was flirtation the actual reason Brian had slammed him up against the pub wall?

I took another slurp of tea, laser-focusing on Oliver's exact words: 'He got all up in his face and told him to stay away from his family.'

Family, not wife. Stay away from his family, and that could mean...Dylan.

Suddenly, I found myself craving the relative safety of Jennifer Werth's presence. I shot a glance toward the door. "She's having a long shower. Do you think she's okay?"

"I'll run upstairs and check."

"Good idea," I chirped. "I'll keep enjoying this lovely

cup of tea." I toasted him with the cup as he stood and hurried from the room.

As soon as Brian was out of sight, I set down my tea and stood. My knees felt wobbly, but they steadied as I crossed to a montage of family portraits on the wall.

There was Dylan, posed in an Easter basket as a baby. Super cute. Dylan as a proud ring-bearer, standing beside his mother in her sleek white wedding gown and his new stepfather, who was beaming like the cat that got the canary. A photo of a younger Jennifer and Brian in front of the Sydney Opera House, each with a hand resting on a gap-toothed Dylan's shoulder. A posed portrait of Jennifer in a graduation cap and gown. And above that, another birthday photo of Jennifer and her sister. In this one, they were teenagers.

My sight blurred as I studied the photo, so I moved closer to see the details. Bent over another bright-green birthday cake, the twins were blowing out two candles in the shape of the numerals one and seven. Their identical clover-print T-shirts coordinated with the green banner in the background. A banner proclaiming, 'Happy Saint Patrick's Day,' with a hand-written sign tacked to the bottom that said, 'And Happy B-Day Jennifer & Julia!'

The clincher though—the thing that made my heart gallop, my knees resume wobbling, and my palms grow clammy—was what each girl wore pinned to her shirt collar.

A leprechaun pin.

An identical twin to the one currently residing in my pocket.

But before I could compare it, hairs rose in a prickle down the back of my neck, nerve-endings picking up on what my ears hadn't yet registered.

Footsteps. Headed my way.

I tried to turn, but it was as if I'd suddenly found myself hip-deep in molasses. Even if I could turn, my brain had floated out of my skull, and I suspected it was headed for the room's double-height ceiling. And even if I could turn, I didn't need to.

Brian's unwashed dentist-office-and-expensive-cologne smell wafted from behind me—a split second before a meaty hand clamped over my mouth.

And then everything went muzzy...wuzzy...fuzzy...

FOURTEEN

When the darkness receded and my eyelids fluttered open, three pairs of eyes stared back at me. Two pairs belonged to life-sized porcelain Persian cats. And the other to a bug-eyed Isabel Burton, the lower portion of her face pulled into a rictus grin by the silk scarf clenched between her teeth.

My head felt stuffed with mohair yarn: fuzzy and tangled with partially formed thoughts that seemed to lead nowhere.

What had I done to deserve the hairy eyeball from the cat statues?

Why had Isabel purchased a scarf in such a bright shade of orange that it made my eyes and ears hurt?

These inane questions ping-ponged around my brain. Followed by some slightly more rational memories.

I remembered someone helping me stagger to a car.

I remembered the motion of being driven.

And I remembered being half-guided, half-carried into an unfamiliar house.

With one sense too many operating at the same time, I

reclosed my eyes, freeing me up to make a mental head-to-toe checklist.

Head? Muzzy and achy-come-hangover-y, but intact.

Neck and shoulders? Stiff, as if I'd slept funny.

Back and butt? Surprisingly comfortable, situated in what appeared to be a squishy armchair.

Legs and feet? Hunky-dory-Rory.

Hands? Still attached to my arms, ha ha... Wait a darn minute! My hands were bound together in front of my body.

My eyes flew open, and I dropped my chin. Wrapped and knotted around my wrists was what looked like a ball of super-chunky, one hundred percent wool in the shade of Violet Skies. I knew this because I'd talked Isabel into buying this particular yarn a few weeks ago. Irony, you are the Queen of all Mean Girls.

Something moved on my left side, and I rolled my head toward it. A hulking Brian Werth lowered himself onto the sofa opposite Isabel.

"She's awake," he called out.

For a moment, my addled brain thought he'd announced this to the faux Persians on the coffee table. Because if the human was awake, it surely meant kibble would rattle into their food dishes like manna from Heaven.

"What? She should still be out for hours." A female voice came from behind me, strident and filled with impatient irritation.

Through squinty eyes, I watched as Brian's face puckered into a scowl. "Hey. Spiking someone's drink is not an exact science, honey. It's not my fault she didn't drink it all."

Honey? That could only mean...

Jennifer Werth walked around the armchair to stand in

front of me, fists planted on hips. I blinked up at her then tilted my head to see around her to where Isabel sat.

Unlike mine, Isabel's wrists were more securely fastened with plastic cable ties. Another cable tie was clasped around one ankle, a second one looped through it and secured to the Velcro straps of the moon boot worn over her injured ankle. There wasn't much chance of Isabel making a run for it, but whoever tied her up—and by whoever, I meant the woman glowering down at me—they'd come prepared for resistance.

Jennifer followed my gaze to Isabel, who glared at her in helpless fury. "Ool ever et uh-ay iv is."

Brian uttered a smug snort. Yeah. Guess the dentist was in on the whole home invasion gig with his wife. Not that there was much doubt at this point. "Oh, we'll get away with this. Don't you worry."

Points for understanding Isabel's garbled protestation. But then, he'd had many hours of practice listening to effectively gagged patients.

"You'll be joining your beloved Lucas soon," Jennifer crooned so sweetly it made me want to take a drill to my own teeth.

Isabel arched her chin and glared at her captor with indignation. "I idn't uv im."

"Yes you did, you poor, pathetically lonely thing. At least, that's what everyone in town will believe. More importantly, it's what the cops will accept as the reason you killed him in a fit of jealous rage."

"I id ot!"

"For Pete's sake." Jennifer strode over and yanked the scarf from Isabel's mouth. "If you scream, Brian will hurt you. He's a dentist; he knows how to inflict pain."

Ain't that the truth, lady.

I snuck a glance at Brian, who appeared somewhat taken aback at the thought of acting as his wife's hired thug.

A bit late for that, buddy. You're up to your eyeballs in this mess.

Isabel licked her lips and swallowed hard a few times. "I did not kill Lucas."

"But you were at the store that night," I blurted. "Ed Hanbury saw you leave the campground, and you were wearing a nice dress and heels, he said." Much like the heels Jennifer wore now: shiny red pumps that coordinated with her crimson blouse. The shoes made her outfit a little matchy-matchy for my taste but were probably quite good for repelling and hiding blood splatter.

"Wasn't me." Isabel barked out a bitter laugh. "Definitely wasn't me. Thanks to my sciatica, I haven't worn heels since my wedding day."

Jennifer rolled her eyes. "Before you two lose any more brain cells trying to Sherlock who the woman was—it was me. It's easier to catch a fly with honey than vinegar, and I needed Lucas to want to talk to me. When he wasn't in his RV, I figured the only other place he could be was the store, so that's where I went."

Where she'd found him.

As my brain rebooted, it started to piece together what had happened the night Lucas Kerr opened the door to the wrong person.

FOREHEAD CRUMPLING INTO FROWN LINES, Isabel huffed out a sigh. "But why did you want to talk to him?"

"Because she'd discovered Lucas had sold drugs to her

son." My eyes flicked to Jennifer, and her hard expression confirmed my suspicions.

Her lips pressed into a thin line, she wrapped her arms around her torso. "I was picking up dirty laundry off his bedroom floor one morning—how the boy can shoot a basketball through a hoop but completely miss the laundry basket, I don't know. I had to crawl under his desk to reach a sock that'd somehow tucked itself against the back wall. Under the sock, I found a dust-covered pill, which I thought was an over-the-counter painkiller at first."

Jennifer shook her head. "But it was the wrong size and shape. So I did a more thorough search of his room and found what remained of his stash. There were only a couple of pills in the baggie, but I was angry. Furious, really."

"You couldn't believe Dylan would take drugs after what happened to your sister." I infused my voice with as much empathy and understanding as I could.

"Exactly. I figured there must be peer pressure or some sort of extenuating circumstances—"

"Like the stress of exams," Isabel said. "These days, kids have so much pressure on them to do well if they want to qualify for the top universities."

Jennifer shot her husband a scathing look. "Brian had been on and on at Dylan since the beginning of the school year about buckling down and studying hard."

"The kid needs more discipline in his study habits." Brian threw up his hands. "Otherwise, he'll end up in some dead-end job, flipping burgers."

Or dealing drugs?

As angry and upset as Jennifer had been at finding out her son had taken illegal substances, murdering the person who'd sold them to him seemed a little excessive. But if she'd uncovered the possibility of Lucas coercing Dylan into selling drugs to his friends as study aids...

"How did you know Lucas gave Dylan the pills?" I asked.

She sniffed in disdain. "The baggie I found had a couple of stickers on it. To help identify which pills it contained, I'm guessing. Lucas sold the same stickers in his store; I checked. I also looked in Hanburys and the stationery section of the bookstore in case they carried those particular stickers, but neither stocked them. But I knew that wasn't enough to convince the police of his guilt. There was only one way to prove the connection. I got chatty with Lucas—even though breathing the same air as him made me sick to my stomach—and faked being an anxious mumsy who needed something stronger than wine to take the edge off. He bought my act and offered a solution, which I picked up late the next night."

She jutted out her chin as if daring anyone to judge. "I didn't take any of the nasty pills, of course. I just wanted to know where he kept his stash."

"In his back storeroom," I provided helpfully. "He wasn't the savviest of businessmen if he didn't understand the unwritten rule of don't poop where you eat."

And while Jennifer bestowed on me the smile of a proud teacher whose slowest student has finally made a worthwhile contribution to an adult conservation, I continued to slowly rotate my wrists under the Violet Skies restraint. The thick but not particularly strong fibers frayed and began to separate.

"That first night, Lucas suggested I find out if any of my friends were looking for a similar solution. He offered to cut me in for any transactions I set up," Jennifer said. "Flirting with me to try to drum up more business, can you believe it?

Then he let slip that I wouldn't be the only one in town helping him. He said he'd secured a teenager to cover the high school crowd."

"He was grooming a teenager? At *my* high school?" Isabel's formerly pale face flooded with color again.

If the cat-faced clock on Isabel's living room wall was correct, by now, Harry would be getting irritated that I might not make it back in time for the first Crafting for Calmness member's arrival. Irritated, but not yet anxious. But even when that irritation turned to anxiety and then to concern, he wouldn't have the first clue where to look for me. Or that I was in danger. Nobody else knew either.

My stomach plummeted into my shoes.

Isabel and I were screwed. There was no doubt in my mind the Werths wouldn't just let us go after this abduction and chat episode.

"For my son's sake and for the other kids in town, I had to expose Lucas Kerr for what he really was." Jennifer slid onto the couch, next to her husband, looking from Isabel to me with such arrogant certainty that I think I threw up in my mouth a little.

I swallowed hard, grateful for the cover provided by the rolled arms of Isabel's comfy chair. Twisting my wrists, I tried to keep any movement below the elbow. "He was a lowlife, scum who preyed on the vulnerable."

"Total dirtbag." Brian, who'd remained silent during his wife's diatribe, clenched his fists. "He would've ruined our live—" A blink-and-you'd-miss-it sideways glance at his wife. "Ruined Dylan's life first and foremost, of course. I understood why Jen did what she did that night."

"You weren't there?" I asked.

"No," Jennifer answered for him. "Brian wasn't part of the plan."

"And what was 'the plan'? Murder Lucas and hope no one would care if there was one less deviant in the world?" Isabel asked with enough venom in her voice to make me flinch.

I gave her a *don't provoke the psychos* stare, hoping that dealing with uncooperative young human beings meant she had some mind-reading skills.

"I'm sure that wasn't Jennifer's plan at all," I said in my best soothing-counselor voice. "Remember, her intention was to expose Lucas's illegal activities to the authorities. Right?" I directed this at Jennifer and Brian, who nodded in unison.

"You acted like a mother lion defending her cub; no one can fault you for that," I continued. If she was anything like my eldest sister, she'd love being seen as a fierce protector of her kid. "I'm sure you just went to Lucas's RV that night to get a confession out of him."

"That's precisely what I did," she said.

"And dressed nicely and took a bottle of wine with you so that he'd assume you were flirting right back and invite you in without suspicion."

"Yes. I had my phone all ready to record his confession, but he wasn't in his RV."

"So you went to the store, and it was dark in front, but the lights were on out the back. When you knocked, Lucas saw it was you through the windows. He opened the door, and you walked right in."

"Told him I'd brought us a nightcap because I couldn't stop thinking about him." She gave a brittle chuckle and shuddered. "That much was true."

"Lucas didn't have any wine glasses, so you used coffee cups."

"Tacky. But it made spiking his drink easy."

"Spiking it with the pills he sold you? Poetic justice, right there." Aiming to inject a tone of admiration into my voice, I kept my gaze level with Jennifer's. "Then, after he succumbed to the pills and alcohol, you hit him with the wine bottle and posed his body on the floor with the chef's knife and a note as a misdirecting flourish. Well played."

I wasn't certain that was how the murder took place, but I gambled on Jennifer's pride insisting that she put all her homicidal little ducks in a row.

"No, no, no." Jennifer sprang to her feet, her cheeks flushed bright red. "That's not what happened." She crossed the living room to pace behind the couch where Isabel sat, her heels tapping out a staccato beat on the hardwood floor.

So far, so good.

The Werths on opposite sides of the room meant I had a chance of escape. Not a good chance, but nevertheless still a chance.

By now, the loosely spun fibers of Violet Skies had stretched enough that, with one sharp tug, I should be able to free my hands. That would provide me with an element of surprise, but how I'd make it out of this room before the Hulk and his killer wife caught me remained a mystery. One I had no clue how to solve.

FIFTEEN

IN THE CRIME and murder mystery shows Harry watches, the detective often impresses his audience of suspects and the hitherto unknown killer with his brilliant deductions of how the crime was committed. My preference was when the detective kept their mouth shut and let the killer run theirs, giving them time to figure out what the heck to do next.

"Tell us what happened, Jennifer." I leaned forward and dropped my hands between my thighs. Feigning interest in hearing her side of the story and hoping she wouldn't notice how the thick yarn was now more fluff than binding. "Did he attack you?"

She paused in her click-clacking stride and turned, facing me from behind Isabel's stricken face. The principal looked like she wanted to puke into one of the potted plants dotted around the room, but her eyes told me she trusted I'd somehow get us both out of this.

Preferably alive.

I hoped that trust wasn't misplaced.

"As a matter of fact," Jennifer said with a darting glance

toward her husband, "he did. Yes, I was furious with him. And it did cross my mind to just secure one of his environmentally unfriendly plastic bags over his head when he slipped into unconsciousness on the couch. But I didn't. Because I'm a good person. A good mother only doing what was necessary to protect her son." She braced her palms on the sofa back and eyeball dueled with me.

"In today's world, teenagers are equally as vulnerable as toddlers," I said. "They think they don't need their parents, but they do."

Appearing mollified, Jennifer shot Brian another glance. This one seemed to say, *'See? She gets where I'm coming from.'*

I totally didn't. I was merely utilizing one of the few weapons I had in my arsenal. Empathy. And years of practice in the subtle art of peacekeeping.

"That's so true," Jennifer said. "My son didn't stand a chance against such a predator, and neither did my poor sister. I couldn't help Julia, but I wouldn't let what happened to her happen to my son. I'd no choice but to intervene."

"You didn't," I said. "And that's why you had to expose Lucas's unsavory side business in such a way that he couldn't weasel out of a prison sentence with a good lawyer."

"Yes!" Jennifer resumed her pacing. "Once I'd found the hidden drugs on his premises, I'd arrange them out in the open, make it look like he was sorting them ready for innocent kids like my son to collect. Then I'd make an anonymous call to the police, who would find him passed out drunk amongst his horrible products."

"Might've worked too, if Lucas hadn't started to come round," Brian said glumly.

"*Would* have worked." Jennifer fired a 'ye of little faith' glare at him over Isabel's head. "How was I to know he'd have a reaction to the pills?"

Brian rolled his beefy shoulders and crossed his legs, the whispery sound of his pants creeping me out once again. "I'm just suggesting if you'd consulted me beforehand about the dosage for an adult male and—"

"Shut up." His wife's face went an even brighter shade of scarlet. "If you hadn't constantly badgered Dylan about grades, he wouldn't have taken drugs. And I never would've been forced to take such measures to save him from someone like Lucas."

A snort of derision from the dentist. "Nobody forced you to do anything."

Dissension among the ranks? I liked it.

"He regained consciousness?" I prompted Jennifer. "Is that when he attacked you?"

She switched her attention to me. "Not exactly." An impatient sigh. "I was in the storage room, going through endless boxes of stock, trying to find his stash. I'm not sure how long I'd been in there when I heard weird noises coming from the other room. Scuffing, gurgling sounds. I left the storage room and found Lucas half slumped, half sitting on the couch, retching."

Her nose crinkled in remembered distaste. "I tried to remove the dishcloth I'd stuffed in his mouth—"

"You *gagged* him?"

"I couldn't risk him yelling for help if he did wake up earlier than expected, could I? And I planned to remove the gag, novelty cuffs, and packing tape from around his ankles before I left and called the cops. It had to look as if he'd been at the store alone."

Fat chance of that, really. Even if her harebrained

scheme had gone off without a hitch, Detective Mana was no dummy. What sort of drug dealer doped himself up and then took a nap among a sampling of his own product? And while the novelty cuffs and gag hadn't left a mark, the packing tape had done a brilliant impromptu wax job on Lucas's hairy ankles. Show me a man who'd willingly do that to himself. However, I resisted pointing out this glaring obviousness and made a sympathetic sound.

"I bent over him and pulled the dishcloth out of his mouth, but Lucas managed to lift his cuffed hands and latch onto my arm. When I stumbled backward, he crumpled onto the floor. It was horrible, just horrible. He was wheezing and choking, wriggling around like an electrified worm." She gave a delicate shudder and clasped her hands between her breasts. "I tried everything to help him, I really, *really* did."

Everything but call an ambulance, which might have saved his life. If I'd had any sympathy for Jennifer Werth before, it vanished at that moment.

Her tear-shiny eyes—which to me seemed as sincere as a kid caught pinching his younger sibling and then pleading innocence—locked onto her husband's. "I told you everything when I got home, didn't I, Brian? How I got the handcuffs and packing tape off Lucas and tried to drag him into the recovery position, but then he lunged at my ankle, and I panicked."

"And you grabbed the nearest object to swing at him. The bottle of wine you'd brought," I said.

If Jennifer's eyes had weapons capability, they would have sent heat-guided missiles soaring in my direction. "Don't you dare judge me, I *had* to. I shudder to think what he would've done to me if he'd dragged me down to the floor."

"No judgment here, Jennifer." I thought my tone was actually quite neutral, considering I'd prefer a close encounter with a tarantula to spending a minute longer in this woman's company. "I just want to understand. What happened next?"

"Well, he quieted down after I gave him a tap on the head."

A tap? The damage she'd done with the wine bottle had looked more than a tap, but I wasn't a coroner; so again, no judgment.

"And I was able to formulate a plan B," she said.

I nodded. "The 'get out of town' note with a knife was to point suspicion toward a business rival or a rival gang, as you later suggested."

"Bringing up the rival gang idea in the knitting class was my little gem," Brian said with no small amount of pride.

What a peach Jennifer had married.

"And that could've continued to lead the investigation in the wrong direction, except you left the cup behind with your lipstick on it, and quite likely, your fingerprints."

"Leaving the cup was *her* fault." Jennifer glared down at the back of Isabel's head. "I'd just picked them up to wash and return to the shelf when I heard footsteps on the driveway. I quickly set the cups by the sink, killed the lights, and ducked behind the island counter."

"So I wasn't imagining things. I thought I saw a brief glow at the back of the store before it vanished." Isabel twisted around as best she could to find Jennifer. "You were still in there when I knocked."

"'Lucas? Lucas? I know you're in there. Can we talk? Pleeeeease?'" She imitated Isabel in a high-pitched mocking tone then returned to her own *I'm the victim* whine. "She wouldn't quit. Knocking and knocking, rattling the door handle. Pleading for Lucas to talk to her with absolutely no self-respect." Jennifer curled her lip. "It was pathetic. I was terrified she was stalkerish enough to break a window and climb in. So I stuffed the dishcloth gag into my bra, tucked the wine bottle under my arm, and grabbed a cup. I could only carry one clenched in my teeth as I crawled out into the store. Isabel was still bleating behind me as I slipped out the front door and headed for home."

"Where I found her beside the recycling bin in the kitchen, about to stash the bottle," Brian said. "She looked at me, looked down at the cup she still had in her hand..."

"The one I'd snatched in the dark that didn't have my lipstick on it," Jennifer said.

"...and burst into tears," Brian finished.

He gazed at his wife with a mixture of admiration and concern. "In hindsight, it wasn't a deal-breaker. Lucas's reputation with women wasn't unknown around town, so the lipstick on a cup could've been left there at any time. The important thing was at least there were no traces of drugs in the cup that remained at the store. And since Jen's never had so much as a parking ticket, she's never been fingerprinted. There's nothing to connect her with the unfortunate incident."

Jennifer grimaced, her gaze dropping to the breast pocket of her blouse. A spot where a woman might attach a name tag for work...or a small leprechaun pin as a memento of her late sister.

The leprechaun pin currently in my pocket.

"Except us," said Isabel.

"Yes," said Jennifer. "Except for one lovesick, lonely woman and a nosy member of a pathetic knitting group who refused to keep her nose out of someone else's business.

And sadly for you two crazy cat ladies, curiosity really will kill the cat this time."

"Murder-suicide," the dentist said. In the same affable voice that he no doubt used to put patients at ease while coming at them with a drill. "It happens more often than you'd think. But don't worry, I won't get the dosage wrong like I did with the mild sedative I gave you earlier." He gave a creepy chuckle. "That's the problem with being a dentist, we can't prescribe the good stuff. But between Jen's sleeping pills and the remains of Lucas's downers, you two will have a nice, long, *permanent* nap. Painless, I promise."

Pretty much the end result I'd surmised once the fog began clearing from my brain. I still felt groggy and a bit dissociated from 'Tessa who'd listened to the pair running for bed-bug-crazy couple of the year.' But two things I knew with absolute certainty.

One: If I didn't act soon, before Brian had the opportunity to cram an overdose down my throat with his gorilla mitts, I was toast.

Two: Worst-case scenario—and my least preferred one—Detective Mana would find my dead body and the leprechaun pin in my pocket. With the luck of the Irish, he'd figure out who the real killer was.

Pity he was no more Irish than me.

Also, out of vanity, if it was Eric who found me, I hoped my corpse would appear more like Snow White than an extra on *The Walking Dead*.

Jennifer moved closer to the sofa back and gave Isabel a 'there, there' pat while keeping her eyes trained on me. "I'm sorry you got dragged into this, Tessa. If you'd left well enough alone after I dropped off my note, you wouldn't have become involved. But when Brian called me this evening while I was busy with Isabel and said you'd turned up on our doorstep, spouting your half-baked theories about my sister. I knew you thought you had it all figured out."

Embarrassingly, I hadn't. Not until I'd seen the Werths' family photos on the wall.

She squeezed Isabel's shoulders as if she were about to give her a relaxing massage. "You forced my hand, I'm afraid. I couldn't risk you blabbing to the police."

I dropped my eyes to Isabel's and held her stare for a few beats until I thought she'd twigged I wanted her attention. Then I deliberately lowered my gaze to her bound wrists before flicking it up to Jennifer, who still stood directly behind her. All the while mentally shouting across the room, *Please understand, please understand!*

"They weren't half-baked theories though, were they?" I said. "You aren't as smart as you think you are. Not smart enough to get away with murder. If only you'd accepted the limitations of your intelligence and skipped university, your sister might still be alive."

A cruel dig, I know. I counted on my inner mean girl lighting a match to what I hoped were her insecurities.

Between bared teeth, Jennifer forced out a sound like a pot about to boil over. Gripping Isabel's shoulders now, she leaned forward. "What would you know about—"

Isabel lifted her bound wrists, looped them around Jennifer's neck, and yanked. With Jennifer screeching and flailing, half pulled over the sofa back and struggling with Isabel, I made my move.

I leaped out of the armchair—okay, to be honest, it was more of a *had a drink too many* lurch—ripping what remained of the Violet Skies off my wrists as I lunged for the coffee table.

And one of the ugly cat statues.

A two-handed grip on the thing's head, I spun around.

As Brian rose from the other couch, I swung the statue, pretending his nose was the softball I constantly missed hitting as a kid. This time, I didn't miss, and Persian met proboscis with a satisfying crunch.

The dentist fell backward, but I didn't pause to assess his injuries. I grabbed the other cat statue from the coffee table and brandished it as a second weapon of destruction.

Sprawled on the sofa, clutching his nose and whimpering, Brian no longer appeared much of a threat. Bigger they are, harder they fall and all that.

I stumbled around the coffee table to help Isabel subdue the screaming, cussing in a most unladylike fashion, Jennifer. Though with Isabel's fingers clenched in Jennifer's hair, tight enough to scalp, she seemed to be doing fine. But just in case...

"Give up, Jennifer." I retrieved her phone, which had fallen onto the sofa cushions during the struggle, and tapped the emergency call number. "If you don't calm down, I'll subdue you the same way you subdued Lucas Kerr."

Jennifer snarled at me through a curtain of tangled hair, her pretty headband hanging askew, caught in a knotted strand.

Showing her every one of my pearly whites in an ear-to-ear grin, I made sure she could see the glossy black cat statue in my hand. "Sucks to be the victim of karma, huh?"

SIXTEEN

To say Detective Sergeant Mana was a teeny bit furious with me was much like saying triple salted caramel cupcakes are a teeny bit delicious. It was just my luck that he'd been on his way to Cape Discovery and had heard about the emergency over the police radio. He'd arrived not long after the first response police vehicle screeched to a halt.

Constable Austin and his partner, Simmonds, had blown into Isabel's house like mini hurricanes. They'd arrested the Werths, with Austin radioing for an ambulance to check out Brian's nose. We could all hear Brian complaining about it at top volume as Simmonds led him outside in handcuffs.

Full darkness was fast closing in, and the police cars' strobing lights bounced off the neighborhood windows as they escorted Jennifer to a second patrol car. I huddled next to Isabel on her front lawn, gripping her hand and shaking so hard my teeth chattered. Dougie from next door, seeing what was happening, had brewed a pot of tea. We heard him arguing with an officer in his driveway about his right as a concerned neighbor to bring over a nice, hot cuppa for us after such a 'traumatic experience.'

It was an argument Dougie ultimately didn't win, but the officer did clomp past with a large cozy-covered teapot. Presumably, on his way to Isabel's kitchen to pour us a cuppa that I wouldn't be able to drink. I didn't like my chances of not tipping it down my front.

Although when the detective climbed out of his vehicle under the sodium glow of a streetlight and stalked toward me, I wished I could magic a hot mug into my hands. Maybe it would have staved off the shivers that resumed in earnest at the sight of his face.

Eric's mouth formed a grim horizontal seam from one side of his clenched jawbone to the other. His thunderous gray gaze found mine and clubbed it with irritated concern. Most likely, I'd imagined the concern, and he was merely cheesed off at finding me neck-deep in his investigation.

Again.

Meanwhile, Isabel moved away from me to chastise an officer who'd accidentally kicked over one of her garden ornaments, leaving me to face the detective's wrath alone. Well, not entirely alone...

Warm fur wrapped around my ankles and a plaintive mew reached my ears. As I glanced down at Pearl's head butting against my calves, another small black shape streaked from the shadows to join her. I looked over at Eric, but he'd stopped to talk to Austin and Simmonds. Grateful for the distraction from his skewering gaze, I slumped cross-legged on Isabel's lawn and pulled both felines into my lap.

"How did you clever kitties know where I was?" I murmured, burying my face in their soft fur.

Purring and bunting were their only responses. Kit and Pearl wouldn't reveal their secrets, but their presence sparked an overwhelming sense of comfort. I sent a silent thank you to Nana Dee-Dee for providing me with my two guardian angels.

Somewhere high above me, Detective Mana cleared his throat, interrupting our love-and-purr fest. But I chose to ignore him in favor of scritching Kit's chin in his favorite spot.

Expensive suit fabric rustled as he crouched in front of me.

Before he'd even opened his mouth, I'd mentally provided him with an opening line: 'Didn't I tell you to back off and let me do my job?' This delivered in an *I'm about to arrest you* growly tone.

"Are you hurt?" he asked.

I looked up, expecting to see impatience but instead noticed his normally fastened-to-the-throat shirt had two buttonholes open, one button dangling by a thread.

"Tessa," his voice gentled, "are you hurt?"

I shook my head. Swallowed what felt like a giant ball of dust bunnies. Cuddled Kit a little closer. "Just my pride," I whispered, and then in a louder voice, "And yeah, I know it could've been worse. And I know I shouldn't have gone to the Werths' house without backup."

Until that point, Eric had seemed in complete control, but now he hissed out a breath and tugged on his collar. The dangling button pinged off and disappeared into the grass. Pearl shot off my lap to investigate.

"Backup?" he said. "You're not a police officer, so who would act as backup? Your granddad? These guys?" He tipped his head at Pearl, who was patting something in the grass with her paw.

"I wasn't a hundred percent sure the Werths were involved when I decided to stop by their house. And yes, my bad for accepting a cup of spiked tea from a stranger." I couldn't help but shoot a wary glance at the officer who'd just stepped into the front yard with two steaming mugs in his hand.

"Why did you go there in the first place?"

I screwed up my face and waved the officer with the tea away. "Will this go in the official report?" I asked after the man wandered off with the rejected beverage. "Whatever I say can and will be used against me in a court of law, that kind of thing?"

It wasn't dark enough down there on the lawn that I missed Eric's eye-roll. "You haven't broken any laws, have you?"

Running my fingertips over the outline of the leprechaun pin still in my pocket, I uttered a nervous titter that wasn't quite a giggle. "Who me?"

"Tessa..."

Tail high in the air, Pearl strolled over to him and dropped something onto the toe of his leather shoe. His gaze shot down, and he plucked up the tiny object between thumb and forefinger.

"She's returning your shirt button," I helpfully informed him. "She has a knack for finding things, though she doesn't often give them back." I dug into my pants pocket and removed the pin. "A bit like me, I'm afraid."

Eric switched his attention from the button—which he shoved into his jacket pocket—to the pin. "What is that?"

"A leprechaun."

"So it would seem." He rose smoothly to his feet with a sigh and extended his hand to help me to mine.

Although I should have rejected his offer, my legs were still a little wobbly. If being a shaky damsel in distress was embarrassing, it would be even more so if I tried to stand

and fell on my butt. I let his hand—his large, warm hand with long fingers a concert pianist would envy—take mine and tug me upward.

"I assume you have a reason for showing it to me," he said. "Other than seeking my approval of a weird fashion accessory."

Not losing sight of the fact he possessed the ability to slap a pair of cuffs on me for withholding vital evidence or tampering with evidence, or whatever other real or imagined charges I could dream up, I gave Eric a modified stink eye. "I'm showing you because I think Jennifer wore it in memory of her sister the night she went to see Lucas Kerr. It must've fallen off in the scuffle and got knocked partway under the store's fridge. Where Pearl later found it."

His eyes widening, he scanned the surrounding area with laser-focused attention. Once he'd ascertained no one was close enough to overhear, he lowered his voice and said, "Are you kidding me? You took evidence from a crime scene?"

"I'm sorry. I didn't know it was evidence at the time."

"You're sorry?" Eric squeezed his eyes shut with a pained expression. When he opened them again, I fully expected to see Detective Sergeant Mana—the Hyde to his Jekyll—had taken over his softer side. And by softer, I meant marginally less inclined to haul me off to the nearest police station.

My earlier adrenaline rush had blasted away the sedative's effects. And now I was coming down from that rush, leaving me exhausted and with no guile left to conjure up anything but the truth. If Detective Mana saw fit to arrest me, at least I could take a nap in the back of his vehicle en route to Napier. "I was trying to help with the investigation. And until I saw a photo of Jennifer and her twin sister celebrating their birthday on Saint Patrick's Day, I honestly thought it was just a novelty from the store—"

He held up a warning finger. "It was. Possibly it'd been kicked under the fridge weeks earlier by Kerr or your brother, or maybe the previous owners left it there. Regardless, the pin is unrelated to Lucas Kerr's death and isn't necessary to build the case against the Werths, given that they've already confessed."

"Okay." *Was I being let off...?*

"Just don't try to 'help' me again. Please."

...with a warning? Yep, it sure looked that way. "Guess I'm more of a Scooby-Doo than a Watson."

With another one of those infuriatingly cute corner-of-the-mouth twitches, he glanced over my shoulder. "Speaking of Scooby-Doo, looks like the whole gang's arrived."

I turned to see Harry climb out of Mary and Gerald Hopkins' cherry-red Mini, followed by Beth Chadwick and Skye Johnson, who stepped from the back seat. Behind the Mini, two other vehicles arrived in convoy: my dad's work truck and Pamela Martin's sleek BMW. Four more Crafting for Calmness members emerged from Pamela's car. Even from this distance, I could see the concern and relief on their faces as they all hurried along the sidewalk toward me.

Sean moved faster than the others, sprinting and ducking around the neighborhood busybodies who'd ventured out onto the street. Without saying a word when he reached me, he wrapped me in a bear hug.

By the time I wriggled out of his arms, ready to reassure everyone I was okay, Eric had disappeared from Isabel's yard. I knew I should probably seek him out and thank him, as shock had apparently stolen my manners.

But for now, I was just thankful for my family and the friends I hadn't realized I had.

SO, how does a thirty-five-year-old single lady paint the town red on a Saturday evening? If she'd recently escaped kidnappers and a killer, and also being arrested, then she might make the same obvious choice as me.

By celebrating the decision she'd made during her near-death experience—not quite a 'knocking on Heaven's door' kind of near-death experience, but still—and having drinks at the Stone's Throw with a handsome, funny, kind man who loves her.

"We won't find a table this time of night," Harry grumbled as I unhooked my arm from his to open the pub's door.

He'd fussed a bit before coming out, changing his shirt twice, worrying about whether he needed a sweater for later, or if the music would be too loud. And maybe we should just stay home and have a nip or two of the good whiskey he kept in the pantry for emergencies. As we'd strolled along the street in the last of the evening's sunshine, my heart had twisted in my chest. Harry couldn't bring himself to just come out and say it would be the first time he'd been back to the pub since Nana Dee-Dee passed, but I felt it in every step. I wasn't forcing him to go—it had been his idea for us to 'have a wee tipple at the local.' But I recognized the tension between wanting to take the first step into his new normal and the fear of letting go.

"Yes, we will." I tugged the door open, and music spilled out. "I asked Oliver to reserve us one."

My granddad's wispy white eyebrows shot up toward his *going out somewhere but nowhere too posh* plain navy beanie, which matched his polo shirt. "Oliver now, is it?" He gave me a cheeky grin. "Why are you out with a crusty old beggar like me, then?"

"You're a cheap date," I said, "and much better looking."

He snorted but didn't push the issue, unlike other family members I could name—*cough*—Mum. I hadn't yet shared my long-term plans with her or anyone else, but after this evening, I wouldn't be able to put it off any longer.

We stepped inside, and Harry's face lit up at the sight of the three-piece band setting up in the corner. He and Nana Dee-Dee had never missed an opportunity to see live music, applauding enthusiastically no matter how the band performed. Oliver spotted us from behind the bar and lifted a hand in greeting before pointing toward a table for two, close to the mic. According to Sean, it was where Harry and Nana Dee-Dee had always sat if they arrived early enough.

I guided Harry through the crowded pub, and as we approached our table, he stilled, staring down at the third chair pushed underneath. He cleared his throat. "Is someone joining us?"

"In a way." I slid out a chair for him then circled the table to take the one with its back to the band. "That one's for Nana Dee-Dee. It'll always be Nana Dee-Dee's."

"Too right." He eased into his seat, surreptitiously dabbing at his nose with a tissue that had mysteriously appeared in his hand. "All this pollen around at the moment. My allergies are playing up."

"Next time, take an antihistamine, eh?"

Harry sniffed, waving a hand in my general direction. "Go fetch me a beer, will ya? Table service is nonexistent in this joint."

I patted his hand and left him to gather himself.

The Stone's Throw was packed tonight, and Oliver was

tending the bar, alongside two of his staff. Although the overall mood was light, the raucous outbursts from the locals' tables were interspersed with the occasional solemn silence. Three of their own were currently dealing with the justice system, while the Werths' son, Dylan, had arranged with his grandparents to transfer to Wellington for the new schooling year.

Mostly, I sensed relief that things had returned to normal. Well, as normal as things got in Cape Discovery.

Dougie stood at one end of the bar, oblivious to the cluster of warm bodies around him, all trying to order their drinks while he talked the young bartender's ear off. Overhearing him complain about the noisy workmen who were tidying up Isabel's house before she listed it with my mother, I felt a twinge of something...residual anxiety...sadness?

When I eventually reached the bar, I caught Oliver's eye, and he took my order personally.

"Breakfast's on me tomorrow morning." I shouted to be heard over the crowd and the pub's sound system.

At that very second, all the stars and planets aligned to provide a pause between songs combined with a conversational lull. I suspect every person in the room heard my offer. And in that pin-drop three beats of silence, I realized no one but Oliver knew that a ham and cheese croissant from Disco's was the *only* thing on offer.

Laughter rippled through the pub. One of the old guys who played lawn bowls at the club as if training for the Olympics piped up from the other end of the bar, "If Ollie doesn't want to take you up on your offer of breakfast 'n bed, lassie, I'll take his place."

Six months ago, in my old life, I would have wished for a passing alien spacecraft to home in on my radioactively hot thermal image and beam me up to probe me to their heart's content. Anything to escape such public humiliation.

But you know what? I'd had a growth spurt since returning to my hometown.

There are worse things in life than being embarrassed. Like being invisible. Like never being embarrassed because you never put yourself out there. Like not knowing the difference between people laughing at you and people laughing with you.

So I turned to the old fella yukking it up with his pals and smiled my sweetest butter-wouldn't-melt smile. "Happy to oblige, sir. Visiting hours at the nursing home's dementia ward start at eight, don't they?"

As his mates roared with good-natured laughter and gathered around to slap his back, the parting crowd left a visual gap in a direct line to the opposite side of the pub. A direct line that ended with Eric Mana sitting solo at a table, studying me with a hooded gaze. In that gaze, I sensed the man watching me, not the detective.

And I had no idea how to interpret my feelings on the matter.

Eric's eyes slid to a spot behind me. Without checking, I knew it was Oliver who'd rekindled the detective sergeant's chilly stare. I also knew, from the tiny hairs prickling along my nape, that Oliver's answering look was just as icy, just as hard.

What I didn't know was why.

But I'd puzzle over that another day.

I turned back to Oliver, who slid two glasses across the bar, and asked him to start a tab for our table. He smiled, setting those tiny hairs of mine reacting in a much nicer way, and said he'd be walking Maki again tomorrow, so he'd meet me at Disco's in the morning.

Once I'd settled back at our table, Harry put aside his glass and folded his hands in front of him. "So, where's your head at, Tess?" he said gruffly. "You gonna head back to the big smoke like Isabel, or will you put up with your nutty family a while longer?"

That's what I wanted to talk to him about.

Even since Mum had discovered Isabel was planning to leave town, she'd dropped unsubtle hints about the possibility of Isabel's replacement hiring a guidance counselor. Me, for example. Trouble was, I hadn't missed the stress—which manifested both physically and emotionally—of working within the rigid confines of high school rules and restraints. The time spent licking my professional and private wounds in Cape Discovery had allowed me to reevaluate my priorities.

And for the first time in a long time, my priority was me.

"I want to stay." I slid my hands across the table to cover Harry's. "You've grown on me, you old nut."

Harry's lovely face wrinkled into deeper lines as he grinned. "Like fungi, eh?"

"Exactly like fungi." I squeezed his warm fingers. "And I'll keep Nana Dee-Dee's store running like clockwork for you until you tell me otherwise."

He grunted. "You've been working for chump change these past few months. That isn't right."

I smiled at him. "It's not about the money. I do it for all the fringe benefits."

"About that..." Harry cleared his throat. "Dee-Dee and I have had a talk, and we've decided—"

"Nana Dee-Dee?" My smile wobbled. "You talk to her often?"

"Every day, now that I can get a word in edgewise. She's still in here"—he tapped the spot over his heart and then his temple—"and in here. I can hear her clear as day, giving her opinion on everything under the sun. So I know that unless I give you what she wants, she'll go on and on about it until I do."

A chuckle escaped me. There had never been any awkward silences when Nana Dee-Dee was around. There was rarely silence, period. I so missed her easy chatter that had soothed away my woes like a balm.

"And what does she want to give me?" I asked.

Harry met my eyes with his own clear blue gaze. "Unraveled," he said. "Nana Dee-Dee and I want to offer you Unraveled."

When my voice got swallowed down in one giant gulp, my granddad continued, "You'll have complete control over every aspect of the business. And for what it's worth, whatever knowledge and experience I've gained over the years. You can put your own stamp on Unraveled. Nana Dee-Dee would love that."

Put my own stamp on the little store I'd come to love? Oh, I could think of a few things I was dying to try. I opened my mouth, then closed it again, tears welling in my eyes. I knew gut-level deep that Nana Dee-Dee really would love me to keep her dream alive. And not because I was obligated to, but because she understood me well enough to know coming home to Cape Discovery and Unraveled was what I truly needed.

At my continued stunned silence, Harry switched the position of our hands. This time, he squeezed mine. "We understand if you have other plans. We wouldn't want to tie you down to such a commitment, because owning a yarn store probably didn't make your list of top career choices…"

Who wouldn't want a career where you got to pimp out gorgeous yarn to like-minded serial knitters and happy hookers every day?

"Yes," I blurted out. "I want it—thank you!"

"I suppose you'll also want your own place, so the cats and I don't cramp your style..." Harry said, but the hope that I'd disagree permeated his every word.

"And leave Kit and Pearl to fend for themselves?" I said. "Their litter tray doesn't empty itself, you know. If I leave, there'll be mutiny."

With a chuckle, he shook his head. "Seriously, Tess. I love having you around, but we don't need a babysitter."

"What about a roomie?" I said, aware of how proud Harry was of his independence. "You're house-trained. There's that, at least."

"I am indeed. It's a steal of a deal."

I lifted my glass, angling it in a toast to Nana Dee-Dee's spot, then at my granddad. "Thank you. Both of you."

Harry dabbed at his nose again. "Should be thanking you for taking the store off our hands. Though I expect I can still hold down the fort while you're off gallivanting in your spare time."

"Here's to gallivanting well and often." I sipped my drink.

As the guitarist plucked out the opening notes of their first song, Harry toasted me in return.

Content, I let the melody wrap around me like a cozy fireside rug tossed over the shoulders. With a pair of devilishly delightful black kitties on my lap.

KNITTED AND KNIFED 197

Want to find out what Tessa and the crazy knitty kitty duo get up to next? Click here to grab Purled & Poisoned now!

Want a FREE prequel of Kit and Pearl's first crime-solving adventure? Click here!

SNEAK PEAK OF PURLED & POISONED...

Chapter **One**

A thirty-five-year-old former guidance counselor, an octogenarian reality-TV-show junkie, and a mischievous feline duo walk into a bar...

Hang on—that sounds like the opening line of a bad joke.

But in reality, that's my reality—minus the felines—entering a bar every Friday night for happy hour with my granddad, Harry. And even then, it takes a spot of bribery to drag him away from his favorite show so he'll join me down the road at the Stone's Throw, where everybody knows your name.

Wait—now *that* sounds like the theme song from an eighties sitcom.

Let me back up a minute before you think you've fallen into an episode of *The Twilight Zone*.

For those who haven't already met me, I should probably introduce myself. I'm Tessa Wakefield, the new owner of Cape Discovery's premier yarn store, Unraveled. We're a small but mighty business located in the heart of New Zealand's sunshiny Hawke's Bay. Let me share some of the spiel I'm writing for our work-in-progress website:

If you're after merino, mohair, or help with moss stitch, we've got you covered.

If friendly conversation and Crafting for Calmness classes ring your bell, you've come to the right place.

But if mystery, madness, and murder make you quiver, then...

And I don't quite know how to finish that last statement because the only mystery and madness I'd encountered, until a short time ago, was my well-meaning, albeit slightly loony family. My life recently took a sideways skid when I stumbled upon my first—and hopefully, last—crime scene. Complete with murder victim. Trust me when I say that the experience was nothing like the crime shows Harry enjoys binge-watching.

For starters, the central character's two cats don't

usually accompany them, thereby contaminating the crime scene. Yes, that actually happened. Now the enigmatic and occasionally charismatic Detective Sergeant Eric Mana has likely stuck me on his watch list of 'harmless but potentially criminal crackpots.'

So, in summary—or in a nutshell, running with the *I'm a bit of a screwball* analogy—from now on, I'll stick with my knit one purl one, adding in the occasional crocheted granny square to keep things interesting. And I've hung up my one-time-only sleuth's deerstalker hat.

The world can thank me later.

Tonight, I had matters more pressing than shady deals, sordid affairs, and cold-blooded homicide to attend to. Like preparing for the first Crafting for Calmness class since Unraveled reopened this past Monday. During the week, every one of our regulars had popped in to ooh and aah over my brother's Michelangelo-worthy paint job and to reassure me that my Nana Dee-Dee, who passed away late last year, would've been proud of the store's revamp.

Fortunately for business, the regulars had also been unable to resist the temptation of all the new deliciously squishy yarn choices. The flurry of sales had almost made me purr with pleasure.

What hadn't made me purr was discovering an hour ago that one of my inherited fur babies had weaseled their way into the cupcakes I'd purchased for that evening's class. Which fur baby, you ask? Kit, of course. 'Bigger-boned' than his litter sibling Pearl, Kit had an ongoing love affair with food. Preferably human food. And yet again, he'd sampled frosting off several cupcakes while indenting the remainder with his paw-print signature.

No longer naive in the ways of my late nana's kitties, I'd leaped into action and defrosted a packet of sausage rolls from the freezer. The pastry now golden brown and smelling heavenly, I transferred the delicious morsels onto a plate, all the while attempting not to step on the eight black paws currently circling my ankles.

"Not for you," I scolded Pearl as she streaked to the hallway door, behind which stood the flight of stairs leading from the two-bedroom apartment I shared with Harry to Unraveled below. She turned and sat up straight, curling her tail elegantly around her sleek body as she let out a solitary heart-breaking mew.

Kit trotted ahead of me, his furry belly swaying from side to side. He too plopped himself down by the door, eyeballing me and meowing at volume as if to say, "Pay no attention to her, human. I'm the one who's starving!"

I hesitated. Harry should have fed them, but maybe he'd lost track of time...

The door to his bedroom swung open, and my granddad stepped out, holding two knitted beanies in front of his plaid button-down shirt. "Which one, Tess? The navy blue? Or the red-and-white striped one for a pop of color?"

He tugged the striped beanie over his mostly bald head and struck a pose. "Not too *Where's Wally?*"

Without one of the numerous beanies Dee-Dee had knitted or crocheted for him, Harry just wasn't Harry.

"Have you been watching reruns of *What Not to Wear*?" Narrowing my eyes, I shot him a sly smile. "Or is this because there's a couple of new attendees joining us tonight?"

I'd swear on a stack of bibles a blush rose on my granddad's wrinkled cheeks. "Anything wrong with a man trying to look presentable, so he doesn't embarrass his granddaughter?"

With a chuckle, I shook my head. "Stick with the navy

blue. That way, you'll slip under Mum's radar; Sean warned me she's planning to make an appearance."

"Lord save us from your mother's meddling," he grumbled before disappearing back into his room.

"I hear ya," I muttered and headed downstairs, the cats hot on my tail.

After a quick stop for a kitty bribe from the container I kept near the store's back door, I shooed the pair outside. They'd slink in again with the first attendees, hoping their cuteness would result in more treats from the regulars. Unlike his sister, Kit felt no shame in performing his meerkat routine or allowing a belly rub in exchange for a treat.

I hit the switch for the store's main lights, and while pausing to admire the fresh coat of pale buttercup-yellow paint that never failed to lift my spirits, I spotted a lanky shape hovering outside. My little brother. Who, at age thirty-two and a string-beany six foot three, was not so little in either sense.

Once I'd set down the sausage rolls on the counter, I unlocked the front door and pulled it open. "Well done. You're *actually* early for once..."

Before he could defend his usual tardiness, Mum stepped out from behind him, her face puckered into its mother-lion-defending-her-poor-defenseless-cub scowl. "Sean's much more punctual now that he's back home with us."

"Hey," my brother greeted me glumly. "Mum came with." Sean gave me a *please kill me now* grimace and tromped over to the counter, where he readied himself to ring up any impulse purchases the class members made that evening.

Ten percent discount in-store for attendees plus a

smiley-face stamp on a loyalty card for every twenty-five dollars spent—a couple of the new ideas I'd implemented. It helped that Sean, when motivated by cold, hard cash, could charm the knickers off even the oldest class members with his dimpled smile and inherited gift of the gab.

While my brother skulked behind the cash register, Mum scooped up the platter of sausage rolls with a disapproving sniff and sailed into the adjoining workroom, set up for the classes. She flicked on the lights, and I watched her not-so-subtle examination of the freshly painted room. Of course, she wouldn't criticize the skill of application, not when it was Sean who'd donned the painter-for-hire hat. But would she approve of the sanded-back and restained large rectangular worktable, the new seat covers I'd run up on Dee-Dee's sewing machine, and the watercolors by a couple of local artists that now adorned one wall?

Luckily for my sanity's sake, she didn't have time to voice her opinion before the first of our regulars appeared.

Mary and George Hopkins arrived with Mary's sister Edith, who'd come to stay for a few weeks. Mary was the founding member of the Crafting for Calmness's subgroup of crocheters—cheekily known as the Happy Hookers. I'm certain she chose the name just to annoy another member of the group: Beth Chadwick, a sixty-something widow completely loyal to the craft of knitting. I was never quite sure what the wee bit tightly wound Beth thought of Dee-Dee's Serial Knitters name, but the gentle rivalry between the groups kept Thursday evenings lively.

The moment Edith entered the store, Harry appeared as if by magic and gallantly offered to show her where the restroom was located. Not quite the debonair flirtation he might've been aiming for, but practical at least, and the shy-smiling Edith didn't seem to mind.

Beth arrived next with one of her 'church ladies,' who was also new to the area. Her replacement false teeth nowhere to be seen, Beth frowned her way past Harry, who was busy chatting with the blushing Edith. Thanks to a goose named Reggie, Beth had flushed her bottom dentures down a church toilet while cleaning it.

Don't ask.

Seriously. Don't.

Get the woman started on the subject of the vicar's pet goose, and you'll want to flush your ears out via the nearest toilet bowl.

Over the next ten minutes, others arrived in small clusters. Mostly familiar faces, but there were also a few new ones. Slowly but surely, our group was growing, and with the chill of autumn looming, I hoped we would expand even further.

Pamela Martin, who owned the boutique clothing store two doors down, arrived fashionably late. Nothing unusual there: the woman liked to make an entrance. Smelling like she'd just crawled out of a vat of expensive perfume, Pamela flicked her immaculately styled ash-blonde hair away from her face with one bejeweled hand. Tonight's carefully selected outfit consisted of loose linen dungarees from her store—with a price tag higher than my annual clothing budget—a striped sailor shirt, and hot-pink felt sandals.

"Mutton dressed as lamb," Harry muttered from where he sat sandwiched between Edith and Beth, who'd snagged the remaining chair beside him.

Pamela swung around, the lines on her face, so carefully smoothed out with foundation, wrinkling again as she frowned. "Did you say something, Harry?"

My granddad didn't miss a beat. "I said, lambswool." He

pointed to her sandals. "Are your pretty pink shoes made of lambswool?"

She glowed under his compliment. "Actually, they are. One of my ex-sisters-in-law put me onto them; I'm planning to stock them in Chic Threads."

After performing a catwalk strut down the room so everyone could admire her shoes, Pamela took a spot at the worktable. She pulled her needles and a super-soft duck-egg-blue merino yarn from her designer tote. "Now then," she announced as if everyone had been waiting for the group's VIP to arrive before they began. "I must get cracking, as I simply *have* to finish this matinee jacket for my darling Archie's christening."

As if she hadn't already gone on about her three-month-old nephew's christening for the past couple of months. She'd roped most of us into attendance, and while I didn't generally have a problem saying no to Pamela, she *was* one of Unraveled's best customers. And since she'd agreed to sell some of the other members' beautiful hand-crafted garments in her store...spending a Sunday morning in church didn't seem such a big ask.

Mum waited for a lull in the conversation and clicking of needles to pounce. "Speaking of keeping flexible"—though no was, and it was classic Maggie Wakefield to randomly change the topic to suit herself—"has anyone tried Shut Up and Stretch's new yoga class, Move It and Lose It?"

As discussions erupted around the table, Mum set down her latest project—a jersey for one of my nieces, in a bulky yarn far too thick for the pattern. Not that she'd listen to my advice—and raised her voice. "Tessa's trying it out tomorrow morning, so she can report back to the group."

I gawked at my mother. *Was I?* "I am?"

"Yes, sweetie. I've signed you up." Mum wore that expression I recognized from my childhood. All I'd wanted was to be left alone to read and craft outfits for my Barbies, but instead, she'd organized whichever after-school lessons made her feel like she was enriching her oddball daughter's life. "I paid for five sessions up front."

Yoga? She had to be kidding. "But I—"

"No excuses." Mum wagged her finger at me. "You need to get out more. Meet people, make some new friends." She mouthed at me, "Male friends."

Oh, great hairy yarn balls.

"Just be grateful she didn't enroll you in that Yoga Au Naturel class they run in summer," Harry said, and everyone laughed.

While I had no qualms about saying no to most people, my assertiveness collapsed like a house of cards when it came to my mother. "I'll give it a go." I flashed her a smile as genuine as Pamela Martin's blonde hair. "What's the worst that could happen?"

WHEN I WAS A KID, my dad used to say, "Ask a stupid question; get a stupid answer." Last night, I'd tempted the universe with a stupid question, and this morning, I was about to find out if my dad's old adage was right.

For starters, how does one even dress for a yoga class when one doesn't possess a yoga body? And when I thought 'yoga body,' my brain conjured up the image of a woman in sleek leggings, a cropped top—which, because the woman had not an ounce of body fat, required no means of boob support—and long blonde hair artfully bundled into a messy-but-chic topknot. I didn't check a single box of my imagined got-it-together yoga practitioner's look.

But knowing Mum would insist on a detailed report, I pulled up my big girl control panties and wobble-reducing Lycra leggings and left the apartment twenty minutes before the class started.

One class, I told myself as I hurried along the sidewalk toward the center of town. *One class, just to get the gist of what goes on, and then I can semi-confidently bluff about my attendance at the other four.*

The recently opened Shut Up and Stretch studio was located on the floor above the real estate agency where my mother worked. I climbed the stairs to find the small foyer empty and the frosted double doors to the studio closed. Apparently, yoga people weren't early birds. Stuffing one hand into the pocket of my zippered sweatshirt, I sucked on my water bottle and tried to appear as if I was a class regular, totally at home in her environment.

Spoiler alert: I wasn't.

From the polished hardwood floor and shelves of rolled white towels, topped with a cluster of fat candles and a squat golden Buddha, to a wall of cubbies filled with foam blocks and other equipment I couldn't identify, this was so far from being my element that I might as well have been on Mars.

Keeping a safe distance away from the equipment—it'd be just my luck to cause an avalanche—I sidled toward a more normal-looking table with a clipboard and pen. After scribbling my details on the sign-in sheet, I perused the nearby glossy leaflets in holders. One was for Grass Roots Health, Cape Discovery's supplier of vitamins, supplements, organic produce and groceries, and environmentally friendly household products. Another advertised natural beauty products that contained mineral-rich mud from Rotorua, New Zealand's most active thermal area.

There were also some less-professional flyers: vegan cooking lessons, a sign-up sheet for regular field-to-table foraging walks, and information about boot-camp training sessions on the beach three mornings a week, starting at six.

Come rain or shine, WE WANT YOU! Snoozers are losers, so zero tolerance for excusers!!! it proclaimed. I assumed the additional exclamation points were to ensure you didn't miss the importance of this statement.

I snorted.

"Something funny?"

I whirled around at the sound of a woman's voice. Rosie Cooper's voice, to be precise. I'd have recognized it anywhere, even in Auckland, where I'd spent much of my adult life.

But here in my old hometown, the haughty tones of my former high school nemesis took me straight back to those awkward early teenage years, when I'd been the new girl in town. Although Dad's family had lived in the area for two generations, my parents had moved to Napier when I was two and hadn't returned to the fold until ten years later. So by the time I started high school, the cliques were well and truly established.

And well and truly closed to the awkward girl with frizzy hair and braces, no small thanks to the popular girls' pack leader, Rosie Stanton. As she'd been before snagging her husband and three perfect kids. Rosie was Pamela's niece, and the apple hadn't fallen far from that snob tree.

"Snoozers are losers," I blurted out.

Rosie scrunched up her pixie face. "What?"

As she adjusted the rolled-up mat slung carelessly over one shoulder by a strap, I couldn't help but check out her outfit—snug-but not-tight-fitting T-shirt, stretch capri pants, and a thin microfleece jacket tied super-casually around her slim hips—and compare it to my own.

Ouch.

I plucked the wandering edge of my control panties from high on my butt cheek, then tightly folded my arms. "Boot camp. Snoozers are losers, so zero tolerance for excusers. That's what's funny."

"Excusers? Do they think that's a real word?" Rosie rolled her eyes so hard they nearly popped out of her skull. "The husband and wife team who run it have IQs only slightly higher than their BMIs."

"Do you even have a filter?" I asked before I could stop myself.

"Nope. I stopped caring what people think of me years ago." She tilted her head to one side, looking ever so much like a curious blonde bird. One that would peck out your eyes if you got too close. "You should try it sometime."

I couldn't think of a response that didn't end with 'you' and wouldn't cost me a generous donation to Harry's swear jar. Something in my expression must've communicated my middle-finger thoughts, and she chuckled.

"You think I'm a rude cow? Wait until you meet our instructor, my butter-wouldn't-melt-in-her-mouth stepmother." Rosie paused, her lips thinning. "My latest stepmother, any—"

The double doors flew open and out stalked a woman in her early twenties. Bar her hair color, a rich auburn that you instinctively knew was natural by her porcelain complexion, she was my imaginary yoga guru. Shimmering emerald-green leggings clung to her long, slender limbs like dragon scales, and a matching sports bra peeked out of the folds of her drapey, twisty over-top. And yes, she'd scooped up her eye-catching hair into a faux-messy topknot, complete with chopstick thrust through it.

I mean, how does that even work?

Cool, green eyes stabbed across the foyer and impaled me. "I'm Josephine, and you're new. You must be Maggie Wakefield's daughter."

It wasn't a question, and somehow, she made the statement sound like disdainful judgment.

Disdain for me? Water off a duck's behind, baby.

But sneer at my mother?

My spine stiffened into a column of steel—probably counterproductive to the whole yoga philosophy—and I'll admit to entertaining fantasies of snatching the chopstick from her hair and going all Egyptian mortician on her upturned nose. But since I didn't want Detective Mana catching me with even a toe on the wrong side of the law again, I reined it in.

"That's right," I said.

She responded with a head-to-toe scan, from my 'just out of bed frizz' to my sparkly flip-flops, and twisted her cotton candy pink lips. "You look like her."

"Thank you. What a nice thing to say." I added a sweet but 'go on, dis me and see what happens' smile.

They would have crowned Josephine queen of the mean girls if we'd still been in high school. Once, she'd have intimidated the heck out of me. But having worked as a counselor, I'd developed a thick skin and strategies for dealing with their particular type of venom, and a now-adult mean girl didn't present too much of a challenge.

Frown lines furrowed Josephine's mannequin-smooth forehead. I could almost see the hamster wheel in her brain spin as she tried to figure out the subtext of my politeness until, with a slight shrug of her tanned shoulders, she dismissed me as too much effort. "I assume you're aware that Move It and Lose It is an intermediate to advanced class? You have done Ashtanga yoga before?"

Ashta-what-a yoga? Um...that'd be a giant nope.

"Of course she has." Rosie rested a companionable forearm on my shoulder. "Tess is as bendy as a pretzel, aren't you, buddy?"

I slanted a look at my former nemesis, who was most definitely *not* my buddy. Rosie owned the Daily Grind, a café that unfortunately sold the most amazing array of delicious food and perfect lattes. Unfortunate, as I was trapped firmly between my sweet tooth and my desire to avoid any interaction with her. But now she stared at Josephine the way I imagined she'd stare at a cockroach who'd crawled out from under her coffee machine.

Huh. She must despise this woman if she'd sided with me.

Before I was forced to lie through my teeth about my flexibility, or lack thereof, footsteps echoed up the narrow stairway, and three more Lycra-clad women appeared. With a final cool glance in my direction, Josephine beckoned for the newcomers to enter the studio and disappeared inside with them.

"She's a piece of work, isn't she?" Rosie murmured. "But she's the best yoga instructor I've ever met."

"And she's your stepmother?"

"Yep. Go figure. My dad must have had a second midlife crisis."

You couldn't live in a town as small as Cape Discovery and not get tangled up in the local grapevine. I'd heard that Rosie's twice-divorced dad had remarried a younger woman —but not that she was at least a decade younger than Rosie. However, I'd paid little attention as, until six months ago,

Kurt Stanton and his new wife had resided in one of his Napier residences—roughly an hour's drive away. Following my first and unpleasant impression of the new Mrs. Stanton, a few things clicked into place.

"She's Archie's mother?" I whispered. "Your baby half-brother?" And Pamela's precious nephew.

Rosie's mouth thinned, and I could've sworn her eyes grew shiny. "She gave birth to Archie, yeah. But she hasn't done much mothering as far as we can see. Poor kid."

Then, as if realizing she'd confided too much, she shook her head and headed toward the open studio doors. "C'mon. Stick with me down the back of the room and try to copy what I do."

Ashta-whatsit yoga? How hard could it be?

ABOUT THE AUTHOR

Tracey Drew lives Down Under with her husband—who's given up complaining about her yarn addiction—and two madcap tabby cats called Kevin and Alfie. The feline brothers constantly battle with her while she's trying to write her books by demanding lap-time, but they also provide constant inspiration for her fun & quirky cozy mysteries.

ACKNOWLEDGMENTS

Thanks to beta readers: Eileen, Hazel, Judy, Julie-Ann, Kelly, Rach, Rhonda, Rose, and Susan.

Printed in Great Britain
by Amazon